# MEET ME AT THE FERRIS WHEEL

*An adventure at the St. Louis World's Fair*
*with 75 authentic pictures For ages 9 thru 16*

by

## JOY DAWSON

Bloomington, IN  Milton Keynes, UK

authorHOUSE

AuthorHouse™
1663 Liberty Drive, Suite 200
Bloomington, IN 47403
www.authorhouse.com
Phone: 1-800-839-8640

AuthorHouse™ UK Ltd.
500 Avebury Boulevard
Central Milton Keynes, MK9 2BE
www.authorhouse.co.uk
Phone: 08001974150

First published by AuthorHouse 2/22/2006

ISBN: 1-4184-3868-5 (sc)

Library of Congress Control Number: 2004094713

Printed in the United States of America
Bloomington, Indiana

This book is printed on acid-free paper.

# DEDICATION

Dedicated to my grandfather, Henderson Cooper Parker, whose love of growing things makes me proud to be his granddaughter, and to my father, Rudy, who was a great story teller. Grandfather's medal from the World's Fair shows his skill as a grower and proves his willingness to help increase food production for all mankind.

Also, a special thanks for the inspiration of James Richard Harter who said to me years ago, "One day you are going to write a book".

# Contents

## A BALLOON-VIEW OF THE FAIR GROUNDS AT ST. LOUIS TAKEN FROM A HEIGHT OF 1,000 FEET

This remarkable photograph is one of the most successful balloon pictures ever taken. It was made by Mr. F. P. Stevens from a balloon at the height of 1,000 feet over the Fair Grounds at St. Louis

# THE FARM

Rudy's horse Mabel pulled the old worn plow as if it had always been a part of her. It was the spring of 1901, and the farm in northern Missouri was beginning to come alive with green sprouts and buzzing insects.

The young 14-year-old was sweating; it had been a long day of plowing. He liked the smell of the earth as it turned over, and when his father said it was planting time, Rudy was eager and ready to take the horse out to the northeast section of their forty acres.

He decided he could make about ten more laps down the field; the skies now looked a bit threatening. As he looped the harness straps around the plow handles and called "gee haw" to Mabel, he noticed a large mound of dirt and grass rise up in front of him. Holding firm to the handles, he steadied the plow because he knew he could not stop the horse soon enough. In an instant, baby skunks were running everywhere. They looked like little bushy black and white beads scattering from a broken strand.

Rudy reined the horse, grabbed a gunnysack off the plow handle, and began collecting the skunks. He had already seen the limp body of their mother, and he knew the babies would die if he did not catch them.

"Hey there!" Frank, Rudy's older brother, called out from the wood fence along the field. "What are you doing with those smelly little critters?"

Rudy scurried to pick up the skunks. "It's a shame, Frank, but I just accidentally killed their mother, and I thought I might raise them myself. Skunk pelts bring a pretty penny these days. Besides, they are so young I don't think they know how to be stinky yet."

Frank held his nose in jest and laughed. He was seventeen, three and a half years older than Rudy. All their lives they had been close, giving each other support. And somehow they both knew they were expected to help care for the farm and their parents. The others had married or left home.

Frank waited for his brother at the barn door where Mabel was being fed. Rudy came out with the wriggling sack slung over his shoulder.

"There are eleven of them, Frank. They are so young—but I think I can take care of them with a medicine dropper and some milk."

"Where are you going to put them?" asked Frank.

"I'll build a pen out of some of that used chicken wire we tore down. When it comes time to sell them, you'll know this was a great idea. They can go to the chick area in the shed for tonight. I'll have to feed them though. They are too small to survive long without food."

Rudy knew that skunk pelts would bring in money he and his brother needed for winter clothes. On the farm, there was usually plenty to eat but getting cash for clothing was not easy.

The next day, Rudy repaired the pen near the old chicken house where the skunks were at night. He was faithful to feed them often until they were old enough to feed themselves. The little skunks acted like kittens and ran to Rudy as though he were their mother. He soon became very attached to the young animals he had rescued.

Frank felt sad because he knew the day was coming when Rudy had to either let the skunks go into the woods or follow through with his plan to sell the pelts.

One day after a few weeks, Rudy walked into the barn just as Frank finished feeding the young jersey calf. He handed his brother a package.

"What's this?" Frank asked, puzzled.

"Open it," Rudy replied, his face mildly flushed.

Frank tore open the paper and found two suits of long woolen underwear that he had been needing so much. The winter before, Frank had been ill and his clothing was not warm enough. He had refused to say anything to Pa. All at once Frank realized that Rudy had killed the skunks and taken the pelts to town. It must have been when his brother went with Pa for supplies.

"Oh, Rudy," he began. "I didn't have to..."

"It's okay, Frank. This will help all of us. I got Ma and Pa warm gloves too and myself a warm shirt and pair of overalls. I hated to do it, but I knew those skunks were there so we would have what we needed." He swallowed hard and added,

"I sure was attached to them though..."

Rudy walked away with his own package under his arm and put it out of sight until fall.

# GROWER AND BUILDER

When he was a child, Henderson Cooper Parker came to Missouri from Kentucky. They traveled in a covered wagon, and his parents homesteaded sixty acres of land in Caldwell County, built a log house, and dug a well. When Cooper was grown, he married Hattie Williams, purchased forty acres near the home of his childhood, and proceeded to make a life for his seven living children. Rudy and Frank were the two youngest.

Some of Cooper's greatest achievements were his fruit orchard and his berry vines. He inherited the interest, for even now on the sixty acres of his boyhood, one could still find large blackberries and boysenberries.

Cooper's orchard included every fruit Stark's Nursery sold—that is, the ones that would grow in Missouri. Rudy had seen his father kill the bores that attacked the trees. With a small wire, he would dig them one by one out of the limbs until the branches were pest free. In the fall, Frank liked to walk under Pa's delicious apple trees. It was a sight to behold for they were some of the finest in the country.

For storage, Cooper put part of his apples and other fruit in the deep cave which had been dug out of the earth and reinforced with concrete. Frank and Ma dried or canned the rest of it. When Christmas came, Cooper spent hours polishing and packing fresh apples and arranging dried fruit for his neighbors and friends. There were few country grocery stores in the early 1900's, and even then, they only sold things like flour, sugar, and coffee. Mr. McKee, their closest neighbor, claimed that Cooper's delicious apples were a feast, especially in winter when it was cold and snowy.

Cooper was also working to get better yields of corn from his fields. He began to experiment with cross-pollination. "Hybrid" was a word folks were just beginning to hear. Cooper wanted to develop a special kind of hybrid corn, and he continued with his efforts to improve the crop.

One morning Rudy saw his father sitting at the old walnut dining table. He was adding numbers on a sheet of paper. "What are you doing, Pa?" he asked.

"I'm measurin' and figurin' a new house for us, son," replied Cooper. "I've ordered all the lumber from Kidder, and I'm expectin' it here by wagon tomorrow. I been promisin' this house to your Ma for twenty years. It's taken a lot of savin' of hog money to buy the materials we need. You sons will have to do the buildin' though."

"Where are we going to build it?" asked Rudy, excited.

"Right out there near the road where your Ma has always wanted it. That's the high spot of our land, and you can see all around the countryside. With your help, it won't be long until we have a new, two-story house."

Frank hurried in from the kitchen where he had been helping his mother with the noon meal. "It might rain tomorrow, Pa. I wonder if that heavy wagon can get through all the dirt roads?"

Henderson Cooper Parker and son Rudy

"Well, let's just hope it don't rain," replied Pa.

The sons knew that their father had talked much of his life about a new home. They simply thought it was a nice dream, even though it was sorely needed. They had patched the old one until it was almost impossible to stay warm in winter.

"I told that lumberman that I would send back any lumber that was full of knotholes," Pa continued. "He knows I'll not keep lumber for my house that is not number one. By the way, did you all know that your Ma is ailing a bit? If she needs anythin' extra or some help, you both see that she gets it, hear?"

"Yes, Pa." They nodded obediently.

Cooper was awake at the crack of dawn. Streaks of yellow and orange were lighting up the morning sky, and the calls of the meadowlarks floated across the pasture. The lumber wagon rumbled into the farmyard.

"Mornin' to you all. Just stack the lumber right here."

But it wasn't long before Cooper had rejected about half of what had been brought him. The delivery men were frustrated and didn't know what to say.

"Here's some coffee, men. I want you to relax and rest. You've had a long journey. But before this day is over it's goin' to get longer. You've got to take much of this back."

Whether it was Cooper's voice or his shock of white hair that stood heavy on the top of his head, he seemed to command an authority that was not to be denied.

Farmhouse that Rudy's father built

# A NEW HOUSE AND SADNESS

The lumber was exchanged and Rudy and Frank began work on the new house. It was a busy time with gardening, crops to get in, and a house to build. Work was from before sunrise and until after sunset. The entire family labored very hard. The nagging worry was that their mother seemed to become more ill as the summer wore on. Too often the doctor's horse and buggy were seen in their front yard.

Rudy felt an urgency to finish the house, and when it was completed, their mother was moved into the downstairs bedroom. Its bright, large window faced the rolling pastures of the landscape, and the south fall breeze seemed to cool her feverish brow.

The day came when Rudy and Frank could no longer deny their mother's grave illness. She was in constant pain and stayed in her bed continually. Rudy heard her moaning at night, and he did not sleep either. A few days before her death, her screams were so loud that Rudy fled the house and went to the barn, covering his ears with his hands and burying his wet face in the hay.

Her funeral was held in a little country church. Rudy sat in the front pew on one side of Pa and Frank on the other. There wasn't time for the other children to come; their journeys would have taken days. Pa would write later and tell them of her passing.

Rudy could not believe she was gone. The minister said they would see her again in heaven, and that they were to remember the good times they had with her and remember all the things she had done for them.

He thought of the book sack that she made him last Christmas. She never knew about the fight he had, and won, with another farm boy over it. And the way she bustled around the kitchen getting meals ready for her family. He recalled the fall that he shot twenty-one quail and took them to his excited mother. She made a celebration out of it and roasted them in a large, black iron pan, along with potatoes and carrots from their cave. Every so often, she and Rudy would open the oven door to test the birds, and he saw her smile at his boyhood hunger. No meal had ever tasted so good, and he felt fine that he had provided it for her and the family.

Rudy remembered the clean beds and the feather pillows she made. She always hummed as she worked. He saw her at the writing desk, for she did a short column in *Capper's Weekly* about family life and other things regarding the home. He would miss her—terribly. But he was relieved that she would not suffer any more pain.

He wondered how they would manage. Frank was the logical one to do the cooking. He had often helped their mother in the kitchen. Frank liked to cook, even if he wasn't as good as their Ma. No one could bake bread like Ma.

Everyone began drifting away from the open gravesite. Many people were there, but they were kind of a blur to Rudy. He did recognize Mr. and Mrs. McKee, their close neighbors, and he saw them talking to his Pa.

It felt peaceful in the cemetery with its nearly bare trees and bent cedars. Rudy didn't like the idea, though, that his Ma would be put down in the cold, dark earth. He thought about what the minister said. So—if he was going to get to see her again, then what was in the ground? It must be her husk—like the green part that covers an ear of corn and is later discarded. She must not be there. That thought gave him some comfort, but he wondered how they would ever get along without her.

The horse and buggy plodded homeward. It seemed to Rudy that the dusk, the quiet, and Mabel's labored breathing spoke heavily of their own emptiness.

After tossing and turning with a chest full of grief, Rudy pulled the pillow over his face and cried himself to sleep.

# DREARY DAYS AND THEN SPRING

That winter seemed the dreariest of their entire lives. Even though they were warm in their new home, there was a chill in their spirits. Their father sat for hours by the large bedroom window, looking out. He didn't do much and sort of left the chores and work to his sons.

Frank did his best in the kitchen. Ma had canned so many vegetables and fruit from past years, that he had a variety to choose from. Rudy knew his father was not eating well, but he also knew it wasn't Frank's fault.

Rudy was repairing some of Mabel's harness in the warm kitchen while Frank washed the dishes. Without looking up he asked, "Frank, where do you suppose Ma is now?"

"I been wondering about that myself." Frank paused. "Rudy, Life seems rather terrible sometimes, doesn't it? I've just decided though that I do believe there is somebody up there handling all this. And if I believe he can create the grass and the trees and the birds, then he will surely have no problem taking care of our Ma."

"I sure do miss her," Rudy replied, his voice trembling.

"So do I, Rudy----so do I. And how Pa must miss her. They were together over thirty-five years. There's not much we can do. Grief seems to be so raw when things first happen, and then that awful sore gradually takes a place inside the heart where it is padded and softened, but it never entirely leaves."

Rudy wondered how Frank knew so much about things.

The winter wore on and each person in the house did his chores rather mechanically. They were like robots, moving about to accomplish necessary living. And Rudy never hated the howling winter winds as much as he did that year.

Then one morning from his bedroom window, Rudy saw a robin sitting in the mulberry tree, singing. Spring was finally here. Off in the distance, he saw his father poking at the earth with a stick in the field where he planted his corn. Rudy quickly got out of bed. There would be much to do.

Friend     Frank     Rudy

# KEEPING THE RULES

One morning, a gentleman on horseback rode into the farmyard. Frank heard the chickens squawking and scattering so he knew someone had come up the driveway.

"We got company, Pa," Frank called from the kitchen. His father was at his usual place in the room where Ma passed away. Frank was glad for any interruption that would get him away from there.

Pa came from the bedroom, through the sitting room, and went to the door. A tall, nice-looking man all dressed in black, even to his boots, approached the front porch.

Pa smiled his welcome and said, "Good morning, Sir. What can I do for you?"

The man put out his hand to Pa and replied, "I don't know, but maybe I can do something for you." Pa invited him in.

The weather had been cool so Rudy kept a small fire going in the pot-belly stove—mostly for Pa. Pa said, "It's nice and warm in here. Sit there by the stove." He pointed to a comfortable chair.

The man thanked him then ventured, "My name is Giles Koger. I'm the new pastor from the church where you had your wife's funeral. I wanted to meet you and get better acquainted."

"Well, that's right friendly of you, Reverend Koger. Where did you come from?"

"I was the pastor for a small church in Kentucky. I brought my family to Missouri because there are more land opportunities here. A pastor's pay won't feed all the young 'uns I have so I do some farming along with my church work."

"I came from Kentucky too," brightened Pa. "Even though I was only a child, I can remember the magnificent mountains there. How many children do you have?"

"Four boys and two girls. The two older boys can help with the farm work. The older girl helps my wife, Bertha, in the house. The rest are in school."

"Sounds like a nice family," replied Pa.

"Yes, and I hear you have two sons at home who are old enough to help you."

Pa kept wondering what the man wanted, but he felt this was a cheerful visit, and the Reverend was pleasant enough.

"I might as well get to my reason for coming here, Mr. Parker."

"Call me Cooper," Pa interrupted.

"Yes, thank you, Cooper." The Reverend continued. "I know that your wife had been baptized, and I also know that you have not. You do profess to be a Christian, but you do not attend church. Am I right?"

17

"Yes, you are right." Pa sighed. "My wife had been at me for years to be baptized, but I never saw the need. I pray. I do my prayin' in my cornfield and in my orchard."

"And I am sure the Lord hears you, Cooper, but there's other rules to be followed." Pa seemed interested so the pastor continued. "The Lord said in the Bible that if you want to follow him and have him hear you, you are to be baptized with water. It's his rule. I didn't just make it up."

"Why do you think that's so important?" Pa asked.

"As you already know, Cooper, Jesus suffered horribly on that cross. His own father, God, told him he had to do that. He was God's own son and God loved him terribly. There had to be a reason."

"Yes, that makes sense. What do you say the reason was, Reverend?"

The pastor moved his chair a little closer to Pa. "It was so we could ask forgiveness for our sins—the ones we did in the past and the ones we're going to do in the future that we don't intend to do. Jesus made that possible."

"Can't we do that anyway?" argued Pa.

"Not without the sacrifice—on the cross. Remember, he said there are rules we have to keep to follow him. We are to receive the Holy Spirit which lives in us and helps us from breaking more rules. Yep, like I said, I didn't write them. Also, he said we are to love one another, especially our families, and do good to all people."

Pa was taking all this in. "Well, the latter part of what you said, I've always tried to do." Pa paused. "I guess I need to go down into the water and keep the rules."

"What Sunday can we plan on, Cooper? We'll do it in Shoal Creek, anytime you say."

"Well, we probably better wait until it warms up a tad."

"Naw, that's not necessary," said the Reverend, smiling a bit. "No one ever caught cold being baptized." They agreed on a Sunday two weeks away.

The pastor left and Pa went into the kitchen. Frank and Rudy were there and both boys busied themselves as though they hadn't heard a thing. The sons had already been baptized; Ma had seen to that. Pa tried to tell them how he felt. He said he wished he had done it when Ma was alive, but he guessed she'd know. He repeated all that the Reverend had said and then told them he had set the date for the event.

"Pa, I think that is just great." Frank was quite serious.

"Yes, Pa, me too," Rudy chimed in. "Will all the congregation be there? We better invite Aunt Sis." He was already making plans.

Pa said everyone was to be invited and that he would notify Aunt Sis. Rudy could go into town and get her on Saturday. She'd want to be there, he was sure.

The day of the baptism dawned grey and cloudy. It was a little cool and Pa was to bring towels and a change of clothing with him. He would wear his white pants and white shirt into the water.

After a long five-mile buggy ride, the four of them arrived at the Shoal Creek Bridge. Rudy helped Aunt Sis out of the carriage and then tied the horse to a tree. They all started down the bank of the creek to where the people had gathered.

It was very quiet, except for someone who coughed and two crows calling to each other up stream. The rustling of clothing could be heard when people turned to smile at each other. As the family approached, Mr. McKee reached out to shake Pa's hand. Aunt Sis was holding a warm, fuzzy blanket to wrap Pa in when he came out of the water.

As the Reverend walked into the creek, the congregation began to sing. He stepped carefully, because of rocks, until he thought he was where it was deep enough; then he motioned for Pa to come out. On the bank, Frank and Rudy were on each side of Aunt Sis, and they saw her already wiping away the tears.

The minister was standing at the side of Pa. He closed his eyes, raised his hand and said something, then he laid Pa back into the water.

The congregation began to sing "There's an Old, Old Path". The sun had not shown the entire day. Suddenly, as the group started to sing the line "---

where the sun shines through", the clouds parted—and a shaft of light fell on Pa and the minister.

So startled was the congregation that they just softly hummed the rest of the hymn. After Pa walked back to the shore, the shaft of light closed up, and the sun was not seen anymore that grey day.

The entire group talked about the experience in whispered tones. At first, Rudy thought he was the only one that noticed the light. At the confirmation there on the bank, when the Reverend and another minister prayed for Pa to receive the Holy Spirit, Rudy learned that most of the congregation had been witness to the opening of the clouds and to the shaft of light that fell on Pa.

On the way back home in the buggy, the family was very quiet. It was Rudy who finally broke the silence.

"Pa, were you aware of what we saw today?" Rudy knew he could always ask his father anything.

Aunt Sis began to weep again. "Cooper," she said as she wiped her eyes, "I can only believe that the Lord is very pleased that you decided to keep the rules. That shaft of light could not have been a coincidence."

"I saw it too, Pa," agreed Frank. "It was an awesome sight."

Pa was allowing Mabel to take her time. His face seemed softer and he spoke with happiness. "Yep, the Reverend was right. That's exactly the rule I was suppose to keep. I'll never forget it. Don't you boys forget it either. You gotta' tell it to your children."

And with that statement Pa said "Get up!" to Mabel and they continued homeward.

# ADVENTURE

The days of the spring of 1902 were full and busy. One fine morning, Pa came in from his walk where Frank was frying eggs on top of the cook stove. "Frank, I got a hankerin' for hog hocks and greens. Do you suppose there's enough dandelion and such now to get a mess to eat?" The ham hocks were used last and were saved for this very purpose.

"Pa, that does sound good. As soon as Rudy comes in from milking, I'll ask him if he'd like to look for some." He was relieved that his father's appetite was returning.

Frank knew that Rudy loved to tramp the woods in the spring. And his younger brother was so proud that he could identify the greens---lamb's quarters, bear's foot, burdock, wild lettuce, and of course, dandelion. Pa thought this dish—a regular banquet. Frank would throw in some potatoes, carrots and turnips, and he knew how to make cornbread. The ground cornmeal was from their own crib. It was a favorite family meal.

After breakfast, Rudy picked up a gunnysack and headed for the timber and the creek. Through the years, there had been a lot of timber cut from their land to keep them warm in winter. They also sent wood by wagon to Aunt Sis's house in Cameron, six miles away. She kept a boarding house for drummers who came through selling their wares to stores in town. There was still timber, but their supply was decreasing. And there was the ten acres their father refused to cut. He said he would buy wood before he would cut the timber there.

It was to the ten acres that Rudy now walked. He flung the gunnysack over his shoulder and began to whistle one of the country tunes he liked so well, "Over the Waves". He had heard an old fiddler play it, and then Rudy played it by ear on his neighbor's violin. He voiced a desire to have a violin, but he knew there was no cash for that. Someday, he would earn his own money and then he might have one.

The air was damp and full of spring. It was a bit cloudy, but he didn't think it was going to rain. Pink and yellow wildflowers bloomed everywhere, and the birds were warbling to each other from tree to tree.

Suddenly the air was split with a piercing shriek. Rudy realized it came from him, screamed again, and threw his gunnysack toward the sky. As he felt the gripping horror, the hair on the back of his neck stood out straight. He shook his right leg until he thought his overalls would rip apart. The yells and leg-shaking caused a confused blue racer snake to slither rapidly into the timber. It was frightened and startled. The snake had been asleep in the warm spring sun-shine, and when stepped on, reacted instantly and wound itself around Rudy's leg.

Rudy's face was as white as chalk. He took a deep breath, picked up his sack, and stumbled away on his jelly-like legs. There was nothing he hated more than a snake, unless it was a mouse. He never told Frank and Pa he was afraid of these things; they might laugh at him.

He continued across the woods toward the small stream where the plants grew. Coming upon a giant old elm tree, and still worrying about another snake, he glanced down in the underbrush. Giving a surprised gasp, he looked all around the ground. He could see wild mushrooms everywhere. And they were big ones.

Morel mushrooms were one of his father's favorite foods. Every spring Pa went out to hunt them. He always said he never found any under this old tree, and he stopped looking here. These were the first that Rudy had ever found. Pa would be so happy, and it was comforting to think of taking something home to cheer him up.

Rudy bent and carefully picked the mushrooms, leaving the root part. He also left two or three to grow so that they might spore the following year. His father had told him that, but he wasn't sure how mushrooms grew. His gunnysack half full now, he continued on to gather the greens.

He found all kinds of edible plants and cut them away from the roots to keep them clean and to allow them to grow again. It took a lot of greens for three people because they cooked down after steaming in the pot. He tried to pick the amounts equally to prevent any bitterness. It was especially important not to add too much dandelion which he later cut from the open pasture. Finally, his sack was full.

He felt it had been a good trip, and from the position of the sun, he knew it was past noon. His stomach knew it too. Heading for home, he held the sack protectively at arm's length. It was chock full of the kind of victuals that Pa and Frank would lick their lips over. Rudy couldn't help smiling.

As he hastened up the slope from the pond to the house, he suddenly called out, "Pa! Frank! Come see what I have!"

Pa opened the kitchen door. He expected to see a boy who was excited over a bag of greens. He smiled his welcome and told Frank to come outside too. Frank had boiled the hocks and was ready to wash the greens.

He took a large galvanized washtub out to the well and started pumping cold water into it. Rudy reached in his sack, pulled out the greens, and piled them into the tub to be washed. Then his eyes began to sparkle.

"Pa, you'll never guess what else I have in this sack? I'm so excited I could fly."

Pa grinned and couldn't imagine. "Well, it must be somethin' good the way you're actin'".

"Come on, Rudy", Frank coaxed. "What is it?"

Rudy smiled and peaked into the sack and pulled out the largest mushroom he could find. It was about six inches long and looked like a sponge. As he held it in his hand, his eyes lit up and he was grinning from ear to ear.

Morel Mushroom photo by Pamela Kaminski

(she gave permission)

Blue Racer snake photo (from an old magazine in Canada)

"Rudy! Where did you find that?" Pa was indeed surprised. "Why, I been huntin' every day, and I haven't seen a one."

Rudy skipped the story about the snake and went on to tell of finding the prized morels. Frank shook his head in awe. Rudy could always find—get—or shoot—something good to eat for the family.

Frank washed the greens twice, then pumped more clear cool water for the mushrooms. They had to be cleaned quickly to get the sand out and to keep from getting soaked with water. With the second washing, he added salt to kill any tiny insects in them.

On the old kitchen table, Frank dried the mushrooms with a soft clean towel, coated them with egg, then flour, and put them in a hot iron skillet ladened with bossie's sweet cream butter. When the three of them sat down to a late afternoon meal, they were very hungry. Frank had done wonders on the pork hocks and greens, mushrooms, and cornbread. And Pa even said the meal tasted like Ma had cooked it. They were grateful for Rudy's provisions too. Frank and Rudy beamed to see their father enjoy his meal, and they all ate until they were stuffed.

---

"Hey, Frank"? Rudy called softly from his bed that night.

"Yes, what do you want?" Frank answered sleepily.

"I just wanted to tell you that if Ma is watching tonight she sure is mighty proud of your cooking."

"She's proud of you too, Rudy. You provided most of that fantastic meal."

Rudy smiled and settled back on his soft feather pillow that his mother had made. He felt very close to her tonight.

# FEARFUL THINGS

Rudy heard Frank scream from the garden. Heart pounding, he grabbed a hoe and dashed toward his brother. Frank's face was drained of color, and he looked like a statue frozen in mid-air.

"What is it?" yelled Rudy, as he ran breathlessly down one of the green bean rows.

Frank was staring at a coiled rattlesnake, one of the largest Rudy had ever seen. The snake was rattling furiously.

"Don't move!" Rudy commanded softly, and he began to inch stealthily toward the snake, hoe raised over his shoulder.

"Be careful, Rudy. He's so big that one bite would lay you up for weeks." Frank was not moving an inch.

Rudy's hoe came down hard just behind the snake's head, and the rattling stopped instantly.

"Whew!" Frank wiped his glistening forehead with his sleeve, shivered, and continued. "I hate snakes—I've always hated snakes—any kind of snake." He shivered again. "Thanks, Rudy."

Rudy thought back to the horror of the snake on his leg. He hadn't realized his brother felt this way too. He pushed the snake to one side with his foot and cut off the rattle with his pocketknife. Frank grimaced again as Rudy cleaned the blade on a clump of grass.

Pa came out of the screened back porch to see what the ruckas was about. "Are the beans hoed?" Pa asked as he walked down the row. When he saw the snake, he did a long whistle and said, "He sure was a big one—about as big as I ever seen. Looks like you really got 'em, Rudy."

Rudy felt good about his heroic gesture and decided he would tell his own snake story when the time was right.

Pa looked up at the sky. "I think we're in for some rain. There's a breeze stirrin', and those clouds are kinda dark. Well, the garden can use the rain," Pa said as he went back into the house. He had been working on his ciphering.

Frank continued digging around the garden plants. They always did better free of weeds and with more oxygen to their root systems. The family was eager for some green beans and potatoes cooked with bacon. Rudy looked forward to the red-ripe tomatoes in July and Pa had his eye on the peas and swiss chard. The food put in the cave last fall was almost gone except for a few jars of canned vegetables and some potatoes. The carrots packed in straw were getting pretty limp.

The wind began to increase, and Rudy headed for the barn to secure the animals and to close the huge, gray doors. It was growing darker now, and even the wind-blown, red-colored chickens were scampering for their shed. Large raindrops were falling here and there. Frank dropped his hoe and ran to close the henhouse doors.

Pa left his farm books on the table and came out of the house to look at the sky. "See that green color in the clouds? That's hail and wind. I'm afraid we're in for it." By this time, Pa was shouting over the wind which was bending and twirling the tree limbs.

Pa motioned to his sons, pointing toward the cave. Frank opened the cave door with great difficulty and the wind blew his straw hat off his head. As Frank pulled the door shut, Pa hurried them all down the six red brick steps. A large toad hopped away from the lower step when the three of them groped their way to the wooden benches made especially for the cave.

It was very dark inside and Pa fumbled for the candle and matches that were kept close by. There was a smell of damp and coolness, and as their eyes began to adjust, they could see the few jars of canned vegetables remaining that their mother had put up when she was alive. The tomatoes were especially colorful next to the yellow wax beans. The bins under the shelves had been full of potatoes, turnips, onions, and carrots. The family was hoping for a good harvest to fill them up again.

Pa pointed upward. "There's a crack in the ceiling up there near the vent that we're goin' to have to repair", he said nonchalantly, trying to ease the tension the storm had created in all of them.

Rudy nodded. "I'll get right to it, Pa—soon as I can. I'll have to dig through the dirt on top to reinforce it from the outside too, I think." They were trying to ignore the noise of the rain and wind, for it was becoming fierce, and even now they could hear hail hitting the air vent.

Rudy rose to go. "I'm going out to check on everything, Pa."

"No you're not", said Pa, motioning him back to his seat. "I think we're havin' a tornado, and your life wouldn't be worth a plug nickel out there."

Just then they heard a roaring noise, crashing sounds, rain and hail pelting the vent, and more banging and crashing from every direction. There was massive thunder, and constant lightning flashes could be seen through the cracks of the cave door.

Frank just stared at the ceiling as though he might be able to see the storm above. "I've never heard anything like this before," he said in awe.

"Last one was when you were a baby, Frank. We were in the old house then. It wasn't a direct hit, but I had a lot of roof to repair, and there was no place to go then for safety. Your Ma was very frightened, and after that fracus, I decided to build a cave as soon as possible." Pa's eyes moved quickly back and forth as he remembered the storm from his past.

Suddenly there was another tearing and ripping sound. The candle went out, and the only light was from the opening of the cave. The wind had blown the door off. The family just sat in stunned silence.

"Stay back in the cave as far as you can, boys." Pa was nervous too. They could see paper, corn husks, and all kinds of debris flying past and into the cave, along with rain and hail. The crashing and splitting noises were louder than ever now, and along with the lightning, the thunder was deafening.

"There won't be any garden left," moaned Rudy.

Pa raised his voice. "That's probably true, but we can replant. All of us will do it and the seeds will soon sprout because the earth will be soft and moist. We're lucky to be safe." He tried to be encouraging.

Finally, the storm began to quiet, though it was still raining.

Pa moved carefully up the steps and peered out. "Be prepared to see some destruction, boys. There's trees down, there's all kinds of trash everywhere, and the chimney on our house is gone." Then Pa began yelling. "Frank! Rudy! Get the ladder and the buckets. Smoke is coming from our roof. I think the house was struck by lightning!"

Both sons leaped out of the cave. There was still rain but they ignored it. Luckily the ladder was left against the old house, but it had been blown to the ground. Frank grabbed the ladder and Rudy flew into the porch for the buckets. Rudy began pumping water as fast as he could from the cistern near the house, filled both buckets and started up the ladder with one of them and handed it to Frank.

Frank yelled down to his father. "It ain't bad, Pa—just a couple of shingles smoking." He doused the area with a second bucket of water that Rudy had taken up. Rudy scurried back down the ladder and began filling the buckets again.

"Pa," Frank called down, "there's a long black streak here where the smoke was. It goes right up to the chimney—well, where the chimney used to be." His voice trailed off, then he added, "Rudy bring more water up here so we can be sure the fire is out." Rudy hurried back up the ladder, and the danger was over.

Pa surveyed the farmyard and the house. The plants in the garden were ruined. Two large trees had fallen near the barn. The door was off the cave, the chimney was gone, and there was trash everywhere. The sons came down off the roof and stood beside Pa.

He sighed then spoke quietly. "Well, the animals are safe and the chickens are alive. Best of all—we're okay. We can sow seeds in the garden again, we can plant more trees, we can repair the door and the roof, but—we can never replace each other. Remember that, boys."

Frank and Rudy each put a hand on their father's back, and they went into the house together.

# GETTING READY FOR WINTER

Spring rolled into the summer of 1902. There were only the three of them now to do the work, and Pa wasn't as much help as he used to be; he spent most of his time in the cornfield. Rudy learned a lot about gardening and canning; Frank became an expert in the kitchen. At times, the two brothers took turns operating the hand-pull washing machine. Since it took all day to wash the clothes, taking turns wasn't so tiring.

When the first frost came, Pa taught them both how to kill the hogs, butcher, and preserve the meat. This was the part of farm life that Rudy did not like. He knew they had to have meat; he knew the hogs had to be killed and prepared for smoking. But he couldn't stand the gun fire, the squealing of the pigs, and the smell of the hides in boiling water which was necessary to get the hair off. He really didn't like the sight of blood at all.

After the killing was completed, the meat was cut and the hams and shoulders kept in the smokehouse over a smoldering hickory wood fire for twenty-one days. The rest of the meat was packed in barrels of salt. Then Pa hung the smoked hams and shoulders in the attic of the house on long wires so that the rats and mice couldn't get to them. The attic stayed cold all through the winter, and there was meat for their morning and evening meals.

Salted bacon came on the slab and had to be sliced off as it was used. The same with the rest of the meat. All of it had to be done by hand.

The winter of 1902-03 was far more settled than when Ma died the year before. The three of them sat around the pot-belly wood stove and played checkers or dominoes. Sometimes it was just Rudy and Pa. Frank liked to read. Pa had ordered a lot of material about the upcoming St. Louis World's Fair. Frank was completely absorbed in it as he read about all the planning for grand palaces and world exhibits. He wished to go there when it opened, but he felt that was impossible.

After while, Frank stopped reading because his eyes hurt. Their kerosene lamps did not afford much light. He knew the winter would be long, and there would be other nights for leafing through all of the material about the fair.

The wood that was keeping them warm was provided by both sons. On one day, Rudy would chop and stack and the next day was Frank's turn. Often they worked together because the logs were so heavy. Both the cook stove and the heating stove were fed with this wood.

Frank learned to add or withhold wood from the cook stove, depending on what his baking temperature required. There was hot water too from a tank that was attached to the stove. It was filled daily. All the water had to be pumped and carried from the cistern into the house in buckets.

Rudy loved Saturday nights. An old galvanized tub used for bathing was brought in. Water was then drained from the stove tank or heated on top in teakettles. He had his bath right in the warm kitchen, and the next morning he could put on his weekly change of clean clothing.

37

See that our label is on the machine you buy, otherwise not genuine.

Pa had grown a bumper crop of apples the previous fall, and when Christmas came, the ground was covered with snow. The apples were polished and boxed, and Rudy was instructed to hitch Mabel to the sleigh, then Pa and Rudy delivered them to the neighbors. They returned with more gifts than they gave away—jars of strawberry and grape jelly, homemade pound cakes made of sweet cream and butter, and small jars of garden herbs, such as dill and basil, that had been carefully cut and dried.

When Ma was alive, she hunted bittersweet for her winter flower arrangements. She knew the vines, and after the first frost, she looked for the buds that burst into two shades of orange. Rudy never saw the house without bittersweet, and the fall that Ma died, he took some of the previous year's vines and put them in her bedroom.

It seemed strange to Rudy not to be attending the one-room school this year where he had attended the past eight years. Frank went until he was fifteen years old, but the duties at home forced him to quit. And even if Frank could have attended high school, he would have needed a team and wagon to go the six miles each way.

Rudy had liked school, especially math. But he knew he was needed at home also. He supposed they were both lucky to have a good eighth-grade education. Rudy could out-cipher any of the other students in math, and Pa had been proud when his son's knowledge was needed to figure so many things for the new house.

Frost pictures on the windows began to melt, and the sun streamed down and caused a sparkle on the icicles. They slowly melted and dripped from the eaves of the house. Winter was almost over.

# FISHING TRIP

One morning in the spring of 1903, Rudy put down his garden hoe and went into the house to talk with Frank.

"Frank, I have the best idea."

Frank was kneading a batch of bread dough and was breathing hard with the effort. "Yes, what is it?" His voice indicated he was busy.

Rudy leaned against the washstand as he looked dreamily out the window. "Do you remember Aunt Sis telling us that fish story last winter when we took her the load of wood?"

Frank stopped to rest a minute. "You mean that one about the time she caught thirteen catfish in the old swimming hole on our grandfather's sixty acres?"

"Yes, that's the one. Well, what if that old swimming hole is still there?"

Frank rejected the idea by waving his hand negatively. "Naw, Rudy, that isn't possible. That's been fifty years ago. And besides, we don't own that land any-more."

"I know we don't own it; Mr. McKee does. The next time he drives past here in his wagon, I'm going to ask him for permission to fish there. If he says yes, will you go with me?"

Frank smiled. "Sure I will, but it won't be for any fish. We won't catch any. I'll pack a lunch and it will just be for a day of having fun."

Rudy stuck out his hand and said, "Okay, shake on it." Frank did, and Rudy took it before he realized it was covered with flour and dough. They both laughed heartily.

The next day Mr. McKee drove by in his wagon, and Rudy asked him for permission. He guffawed loudly and was even more doubtful than Frank was. He vowed there weren't any fish in that small creek, but he was sure willing to allow those two boys to try to catch some.

Everyone said there were no fish; Rudy probably should listen. However, he shrugged off all doubts and made plans for the day.

He took a cane fishing pole, some string, a number of different sized hooks, and a can of worms that he dug. Frank took the picnic lunch. They were to have leftover cold mashed potato sandwiches with grape jelly on them, a couple of apples from the cave, and two pieces of cake that a neighbor had brought over. The ham and bacon had been eaten long ago, and there would not be more until killing time in the fall. It would be an occasional "chicken in the pot" from now on.

"Here's the spot," said Rudy. There was no big hole to speak of and Rudy's face fell.

Frank tried to be encouraging, even with all his doubts. "Are you sure you have the right place, Rudy?"

"Yes, this is how Aunt Sis described it. See that huge oak on the other side of the creek, the one with the fork about half-way up? This is the place. She said they

42

used to swing on a rope out from that tree and let go and drop into the water. The stream here then was about ten feet deep."

"I hate to say it, Rudy, but it sure isn't ten feet deep now. I'd say it is more like one foot." Frank began to laugh. He just couldn't help himself. He laughed so hard that Rudy began to laugh with him. They laughed and laughed as they rolled in the grass, making all kinds of silly comments, until their sides hurt.

It was time for lunch, and Frank began to unpack his sack and they ate. "Okay, so I had a silly dream," admitted Rudy as he sat on the grass finishing his last bit of cake. He suddenly got to his feet. "I think I will take a walk upstream and see what is there."

"And I think I'll take a nap here in the warm sunshine. This is really peaceful after all the chores at the house."

Rudy left Frank sprawled out on the ground. He took his fishing pole and pushed through the brush close to the bank. Frogs leaped into the shallow puddles as he moved along, and he wondered what this stream was really like many years ago.

He walked about a half a mile and was surprised to find a large area of water. It looked promising, though he had no idea how deep it was. It seemed to be cut off from the rest of the stream except he could see a trickle of water flowing in and water flowing out. He knew rainfall had been light. Was it possible that some fish had been trapped in this hole?

He decided to cast in his line. He slid a cork bobber about three feet from the hook. He put a worm on the hook and flung it out to the middle of the stream. Nothing happened and he let his mind wander.

Suddenly there was a great jerk and the bobber was gone. Rudy screamed for Frank. But Frank was much too far away and sound asleep.

He pulled on the pole, trying to be careful not to break the line. It zigzagged back and forth across the pool, and Rudy wondered what he could possibly have. Could it be a turtle? It seemed too active for that. Once the pole bent double and was almost jerked out of his hand. His heart was really pumping. Maybe this was his fish of fishes. Maybe this was the big one.

After fighting the thing a long time, it finally began to tire. Rudy laid the pole on the bank, grabbed the line with his hands, and pulled it in, inch by inch. Whatever was on the other end was so strong that he could do no more than that.

At last he was able to see something. It was a head—it was a huge, blue looking head with whiskers. What a fighter!

Rudy waded into the water to get closer to what was possibly a monster. As he grabbed for his catch, he got finned on his thumb, but ignored it and grabbed again. The gill was exposed, and he put his thumb and forefinger through the mouth and gill and pulled with all his strength. He fell backwards in the water, and the large fish still connected to the pole and line, landed on the bank. It flopped and flipped in the dirt and leaves.

Rudy found a stick, put his foot on the fish's tail, and propped open its mouth to remove the hook. He then cut a large piece of grapevine and made a leader for carrying it. By this time the fish was mostly subdued.

The wet and panting fisherman sat on the bank and looked at his prize. He thought it weighed no less than seven pounds. Seven pounds! Wouldn't Frank be surprised.

It wasn't easy to carry, especially with his pole and can of worms. He decided to leave the worms.

Frank was still asleep when he returned. Rudy laid the blue catfish beside Frank's arm and sat and grinned. Frank awoke to giant whiskers, and leaped off the grass with a start.

"Well, what do you say now, Brother dear?" Rudy was ready to really rub it in.

"Gee, who would have believed it!" exclaimed Frank, now very much awake. "It's a big blue. I can't imagine how a catfish that large got into this little stream. He must have been caught in a pool and couldn't do anything but eat his way into being a prizefighter. Maybe he's related to the great boxer, John Sullivan, except John was probably never as wet as you are, Rudy." Humor was Frank's way of dealing with his brother's teasing remarks.

Rudy's hunger knew a good meal was coming. "How do you think you will cook him, Frank?"

**Blue catfish**

Catfish usually have two to four pairs of whiskers. The small glass catfish is popular in home aquariums. The blue catfish is a food fish found in the Mississippi Valley. The armored catfish is protected from enemies by overlapping bony plates.

"Since he is so large, I think I'll bake him with some home-canned tomatoes, onions, garlic, herbs and a little vinegar. How does that sound?" Frank knew he was in charge now.

"M-m-m-m! I can't wait. What else are we going to have?" The boys were walking back across the field with their dangling fish.

"Perhaps some of those new little potatoes out of the garden with fresh peas. And, of course, slices of my homemade bread."

"I'm sure glad you know how to cook, Frank."

"I'm glad you are a good fisherman, Rudy."

They grinned at each other and walked side by side toward home.

# AN EXCITING SWIM

During the summer of 1903, Cooper was again occupied with his hybrid corn. He had been working on it a few years now, and he seemed pleased with the results. He was getting greater yields, and the kernels filled up the large cob right to the tip.

Rudy watched his father, so intent on his corn growing. Why did he feel that Pa was planning something—something big? Pa seemed driven, as if he was on a time schedule. These thoughts came only occasionally, but he did wonder about it.

While Pa was in the cornfield, Rudy and Frank were busy with other things. Frank was weeding the garden, and Rudy was working on the crack in the ceiling of the cave. It was a hot and humid day.

Rudy stuck his head out of the cave and shouted to Frank in the garden. "Frank, I'm sweating all over. Let's take a swim in the pond. I need a break."

Frank straightened up from his hand-weeding and said, "What a good idea, Rudy. You know, I don't even care that those cows are in there." He added with a grin, "And they have probably been doing their business in there too." They laughed and each grabbed an old pair of cut-off overalls and headed for the pond.

The pond had been built at the bottom of the hill. There was no spring to feed it, only run-off water, and it was usually quite muddy.

"Frank, how deep do you suppose the water is now?"

"Oh, about fifteen feet in the deepest part. Over our heads. Are you afraid of the water?"

Rudy was afraid of water. He had few chances to learn to swim and was not very sure of himself. He did not want to admit it to his brother, though. Frank was a good swimmer.

"I think I'll get some jugs out of the old house," ventured Rudy. "If we put corks in them and tie two together, they should make great floats. We won't even have to swim; we can just lie back in the water and take it easy. Do you want a couple of jugs, Frank?"

Cooper had purchased some ceramic jugs at a farm sale years ago. He thought they would be useful for syrup or other things. Frank did not want to hurt Rudy's feelings. "Sure, that would be fun; go ahead and get them."

In the old house that was used for storage now, Rudy found some heavy twine and looped it through the jug handles. He got the corks out of a drawer in a cabinet. With a set of jugs in each hand, he ran down the hill to the pond where a couple of jersey cows and one holstein were standing near the edge of the water.

"Move over, bossies," Rudy said, as he slipped his pair of jugs under his arms. "You have had this pond all to yourself too long."

As Rudy handed the other pair of jugs to his brother, he felt the cool water flow over his arms. "Never has anything felt so great," sighed Rudy. "Couldn't you just stay here all day, Frank?"

The brothers kicked the water and yelled with delight. The cows just looked at them and went on chewing their cuds. Frank swam across the pond, pulling his jugs after him.

Rudy kicked out farther and decided to turn over on his back. When he did, the cork came out of one jug and floated away. Rudy did not see it at first, and then he tried to recover it. The twine came away from under his arm; the uncorked jug was already going to the bottom and it pulled the other jug with it.

Rudy was frightened. He knew how to tread water a little, but he was so scared he was not thinking. He began to flail his arms and yell to Frank who was at the other end of the pond.

"Frank! Frank! I lost the jugs, and I don't think I can stay up!" Then Rudy went under.

Frank threw his jugs upon the bank and swam as fast as he could out to the middle of the pond. He had to reach Rudy in time, and he was in a panic thinking about it. He had just lost Ma. He couldn't bear to lose his brother too.

When Frank reached the place where Rudy went down, he could not locate him—not even with his feet. He decided to dive for him. Deep into the murky depths he opened his eyes, but the water was so muddy he could see nothing.

He surfaced quickly, thinking Rudy would come up again. He did, but Frank was too far from him, and he went down a second time. He swam toward him, swirling the water like a madman doing a wild ballet, and then suddenly his foot touched Rudy's head.

Reaching down with all his might, he grabbed Rudy by the hair, spitting and gasping for air himself, and pulled him to the surface. Rudy wasn't moving, and Frank secured him under his arm and swam hard, pulling him to shore.

He wasn't certain what to do next. Pa once told a tale of a mother who turned her little girl over on her stomach and pushed on her lungs from the back and saved her. He rolled his brother over—face to the side.

As Frank worked over Rudy, he thought about the day his brother was born. How glad he had been, a three and a half year old, to know he was going to have someone to play with. He'd stand by Rudy's crib, wishing he would grow faster. Though he was very young, he could clearly remember that event. He jerked himself back and looked at Rudy's face.

It didn't have much color, and then Frank saw some water draining from his mouth, but there was still no sign of air.

Frank pumped his back again furiously. "Come on, Rudy, breathe! Rudy do you hear me? I can't take care of Pa and the farm by myself. You have to live! And besides, Rudy, I love you, and you just have to live!" Frank was close to being hysterical.

Rudy began to sputter and mumble between gasps. "What are you shouting about, Frank? Cough! Cough! For pete's sake, I'm not deaf! And what are you doing on my back?"

Frank put his face in his hands, rolled over on to the bank of the pond, and sobbed with relief.

# JANUARY - 1904

January of 1904 passed uneventfully. Now that the family was more adjusted to Ma being gone, they almost looked forward to the cold months; it was a time of rest.

The wood was cut and stacked, and they could leisurely eat what they had grown and preserved from the summer before. It was also a time for more reading, playing games, and listening to Pa's stories. Frank continued to pour over the information about the forthcoming 1904 World's Fair. There was new material he hadn't seen.

Sometimes during winter, Rudy and Frank went out for a walk or a snowball fight. They always checked on the animals, seeing that their stalls were clean and filled with fragrant hay.

Frank did a lot of cooking: stews, biscuits, breads, and pancakes. When Frank was bored, he cooked. Rudy claimed he always gained weight during winter.

One evening, about dusk, it began to snow. It was the kind of feather-like snow that drifts slowly from the skies, with no sound and no wind. Frank appreciated the warm clothing that Rudy had previously provided him; he could now be outside in the cold when he wished.

The snow was soft and the flakes were huge. For some reason, it brought Frank a sense of peace. As he walked, he felt he was floating under a canopy of white. He reflected on the times his family had been together, and especially when

Ma was with them. He decided that whether they were all here or somewhere else, even Ma, they were still a family.

Frank reluctantly went back into the house and to bed, but his eyes would not close. He rolled over and looked out of the window. It had stopped snowing. He saw the moon slide out from a wispy cloud. It's brightness lighted the earth and showered diamonds across the snow. Frank remained almost sleepless that hallowed night.

And nature can usually be depended upon; the snowdrifts melted. The robins returned and built their nests and sang loudly over a hatched blue egg. Spring once again came to the farm.

## WINTER EVENING IN THE WOODS

It has been said that the Swedish painters do not paint true to nature, that they exaggerate the color of their pictures, giving to their composition a chromatic quality and range not to be seen in the actual landscape of Sweden. Be that as it may, the Swedish artists have no need to apologize for their color schemes. Take for example the work of Ansheim Schultzberg, that marvelous interpreter of Scandinavian landscape. Seven of his canvases adorn the walls of the Swedish section in the east pavilion of the Palace of Fine Arts, and the same quality is to be found in all of them. "Winter Evening in the Woods" is one of the most charming. It is a wood interior in the dead of winter, the interior of a pine forest, the branches of the thickly set trees drooping with their weight of snow. The earth is piled with soft drifts of the same snow, gray-purple in the shadow and touched with life where the light from a perfectly glorious after-glow filters through the dense foliage. The glory of the picture is this western sky that gleams through the interstices of the forest wall. And the painter who was capable of putting the high light in the background and yet of making all the elements of his composition keep their place was working with the brush of a master.

# A BIG SURPRISE

The spring of 1904 was one of great excitement. The sons were now seventeen and twenty, more grown up in many ways. Cooper Parker declared he had a corn that would increase yields by fifty percent. Pa had secretly been one of the winners with his corn at the county seat, and Caldwell County was going to send some of his prize ears to be judged in the Missouri section in the Agricultural Building at the St. Louis World's Fair.

After telling the sons about this, Pa had something startling to announce. Frank and Rudy were being sent to the fair to enjoy all the sights and to witness the results of the judging.

The brothers were ecstatic. They had never been to a large city before, let alone a world's fair. They talked of nothing else, even though their trip was months away, and they were full of questions.

"How do we get there, Pa?" Rudy wanted to know. "It will take money, Pa?" He could not see it happening.

"Pa, we don't have clothes to go to a big city! What will those folks say? Where will we stay?" Frank was baffled. How could Pa accomplish this?

"Now boys," Pa said, "don't worry about it. I have been plannin' a long time. I sent away two years ago for the information. You've been reading some of it, Frank. By the way, President Theodore Roosevelt has already dedicated the fair; it was on April 30, 1903 in the Palace of Liberal Arts. Anyway, you'll go in the fall when the judging takes place. I've been savin' for this. I knew I could never go—got too much to do. You sons are the ones who should see such a grand event. You'll go on the train to the city, and you will stay with your older brother, Fred. Though you don't remember him probably, he has agreed, by letter, to keep you while you are there." He sighed and looked away. "I don't know how his wife will feel about this, but Fred will see to it that you're taken' care of." Pa was almost as excited as his sons were, and he refused to allow his worry over Francine to shadow what was happening.

Rudy shook his head in disbelief. "So that is why you have spent so much time in the cornfield?"

Pa nodded. "Yes, and what I've learn't must be shared with others. It's important to the world, boys. We seem to be the country that must help people feed themselves. This here corn will aid in that purpose, and I want to be a part of it. And you sons must learn all you can about everythin' while you're there."

One day a package arrived from a catalog store. It contained two tailored suits, four shirts and other special clothing for Frank and Rudy. They knew Pa had ordered them. The suits were dark and handsome, and the white shirts very stylish.

"Now sons," Pa began, "we'll put these clothes away until the big day. Try them on and see if they fit. We still have time to send them back if they don't."

Palace of Liberal Arts

Where President Teddy Roosevelt

Dedicated the Fair

Frank and Rudy wondered how their father knew so much about sizes. The clothes fit perfectly, and they couldn't wait to wear them. There were even new black shoes and each son had a black bowler hat. Oh, they were going to be quite dapper in that great metropolis of a city.

Clothing worn by Frank and Rudy to the fair.

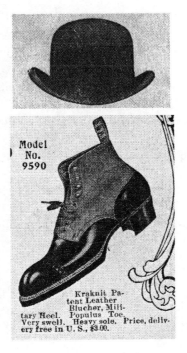

Model
No.
9590

Kraknit Pa-
tent Leather
Blucher, Mili-
tary Heel. Populus Toe.
Very swell. Heavy sole. Price, delivery free in U. S., $3.00.

Frank and Rudy's new bowler hat and new shoes.

# THE JOURNEY

The day finally came. During the summer and early fall, the sons had tried to keep their excitement in check. After all, they still had the usual work to do, but somehow they were able to contain themselves and take care of the farm. They wanted to be sure their father would not have any extra to do when they were not there. Now, their valises had been packed and they were waiting at the train station with Pa.

Pa had already purchased their round-trip tickets. He continued to give them last minute counseling. "Be sure and get all the information about the judgin', Frank. And Rudy, you help your brother, Fred, and Francine. Be sure you give them my regards—both of them. Careful of your money and keep it in your front pockets. Just remember everythin' about the fair so you can come back and tell me."

When the Burlington train pulled in, Pa was still thinking of things to tell his sons. "Come on, Rudy," Frank said, pulling his brother to the coach platform and on to their seats. As the train blew its whistle and steamed noisily away, the boys waved goodbye to their father. Rudy thought Pa looked a little forlorn standing there all by himself.

"Frank, I can't believe we are really riding a train. Say, do you remember Fred? I don't, but I hope he meets us."

"Yes, I remember him—vaguely. He is fifteen years older than I am. There was a problem in the family when he wanted to marry. He begged Pa to give him his inheritance and Pa said he could not do that yet. Fred kind of felt his wife was above us socially, and I guess he wanted to give her things. She's French and part of the St. Louis elite. Fred hasn't been home since. Ma used to tell me these things, but she didn't hold no grudge. I hope there won't be any trouble with Francine. If Pa contacted them, I guess he wanted us to attend the fair real bad."

Rudy was listening to Frank but was also intrigued with the sights he was seeing out of the train window.

"Look, Frank, those people have such a herd of cattle, it makes me wonder how they care for all of them."

But Frank was busy gazing at the beautiful young ladies on the train. There were so many in one place and all with escorts. Of course, Frank knew that no lady went anywhere by herself. They were dressed in gorgeous long dresses of navy, black or gray satins or brocades. And the hats! Never had he seen such hats---all feathers and ribbons and with soft faces under them. Frank gulped and decided this was already a different world than he was used to. He was glad their Pa had outfitted them so handsomely for the fair.

Ladies on the train.

After hours of looking out of the window, they finally arrived in St. Louis. Fred met them at the station and helped them with their valises. He seemed glad to see them, and as they climbed into Fred's new Model C Schacht car, Rudy seemed to go crazy. He kept asking questions about the car since he had not even seen one before. Fred smiled at Rudy's enthusiasm and was glad they both had come. Frank told Fred about Ma's passing and about Pa and his hybrid corn. It seemed easy for them to talk to their brother, as though they had always known him.

When they arrived at the house, Fred seemed a little nervous. "Dear— Francine, we're here," he called out. "These are my brothers from Kidder, and they have come all the way to see the fair and to see Pa's entry in the Missouri exhibit."

Francine was a beautiful woman. She was tall and slender, and like many of the French, she had dark hair and blue eyes. Frank thought her face was of fine porcelain, which seemed in complete harmony with the lovely Victorian home she had decorated in red and pink velvet. He could understand his brother Fred's desire to spoil her.

She walked toward them with her hand outstretched and greeted the brothers. "I have a nice sandwich supper all ready for you on the sideboard." As she led the way, she motioned for them to follow.

They filled their plates and sat down at the table. Rudy was hungry. While they ate, Francine asked them about their trip, their father—was he well—she offered grave sympathy for the passing of their mother, then asked them questions about their ages and well-being. Rudy liked the way she held her tea cup, so daintily and careful. He watched everything she did, then he was able to feel more comfortable with a white napkin across his lap, a silver teapot at his elbow, and flowers on the linen tablecloth. She said the flowers were red mums out of her own garden.

Frank asked Fred to direct him to the fairgrounds. Fred explained where they could catch the horse-drawn trolley, how much to pay, and when to get off at the main entrance. He discussed the price of admission, asked them if they had funds, to which they assured him Pa had taken care of all that. Fred was a little amazed to find that his brothers knew so little about a city, but then they had lived their entire lives on the farm.

It was quite late when they all finally decided to quit visiting and get some much-needed rest.

The car Fred purchased

Francine Parker

Model "A"—Single Seat, without Top.                    Price, $950.00.

2727 Spring Grove Avenue,          CINCINNATI, OHIO, U. S. A.

Another model of the Schacht car.

# THE FANTASTIC 1904 WORLD'S FAIR

The next morning Rudy awoke with a start. He looked at Frank and saw that his eyes were open. "Frank, did you sleep any last night?"

"I did not. It wasn't because of the bed either. I never felt such a soft bed. No, it's our visit today to the fair, and I—I kept seeing those pretty girls on the train. They were so happy and so lovely. I think I am growing up, Rudy."

Rudy had to laugh. "Well, don't act like it's a disease or something. It's probably normal for you to start thinking about girls. Not me, I've got too many other things to think about. I did notice Francine, though. Isn't she pretty?"

"Yeah, and Fred is very lucky. Looks like he provides her with a fantastic living, though. I think he is an executive for a meat packing business. He'd have to be, to have that new car and this beautiful home. And you know what, Rudy? I think Francine likes us more than she'd planned to."

Rudy threw back the covers and leaped out of bed. "Well, what's not to like? We're going to be two of the best-looking young men at the fair, aren't we? So, Frank come on and get ready. I can't wait to get there."

Francine had breakfast ready for them when they arrived downstairs. Her eyes lit up when she saw how handsome they looked and told them so. She was dressed in a lovely morning gown, all shiny and blue, and she had left eggs, bacon, toast and coffee on the sideboard for them. She excused herself while wishing them a pleasant day, saying she was late for an appointment, and that she would see them for supper. Fred had already left.

Riding the trolley was the beginning of a day of firsts. The street they were on was covered with some kind of black-looking tar. None of the roads they were ever on were covered with anything—they were all dirt—and quite muddy when it rained. This street was smooth and easy to ride on. There were horse-drawn carriages and buggies everywhere, and even single riders. They saw a car or two and stretched their necks to watch them as long as they could. They had never seen such an exciting place.

Frank was amazed at the stores and the clothes and goods in the windows. He wondered how much some of these things cost, and then wondered who in the world had enough money to buy them. He guessed Fred did—so there had to be others.

They reached the main gate of the fairgrounds and made their way to the ticket booth. Seeking direction, they were handed a map with their tickets. They went through the gates and could not believe what was before their eyes. As far as they could see there were huge white buildings, tall statues, water, boats, and waterfalls. And each space was dotted with people of every culture, dress, shape, and gender. There were crowds beyond anything they had ever experienced.

"Frank, there are so many people in one place! I'm glad we arrived early. What are all these buildings?"

Actual trolley-ticket to the fair.

"I'm looking at the map, Rudy. Let's get to that other end to see the waterfall. That looks like a good place to begin." They noticed that where they walked and on either side of the large Basin were beautiful maple trees.

As the two brothers moved into the fairgrounds they didn't talk much. Each was too busy trying to absorb what they were seeing. All around them were the grandest buildings and statues ever. Rudy never knew such things existed, and Frank had only seen a few of these things in pictures.

They finally arrived at the Colonnades. "Frank, touch this column. It is cold and white and lovely with the statue in the center. I guess it represents Louisiana. That's what it says. This is incredible!" They walked past more columns which were engraved with the names of other states. Frank explained that he had read about the buildings; some were permanent and others were constructed of pine,
covered with white plaster and fibers. Now he knew why the fair was also called the "Ivory City". It looked like a great expanse of white marble.

Festival Hall with its ornate dome had been built in the middle of the Colonnades. Frank pointed to the building and said, "Rudy, there is a grand pipe organ in that hall. The auditorium there seats 3500 people. I would like to hear the music, but it is not being played now. Maybe we can come back later."

From off the front of Festival Hall, there issued a vast, bubbling waterfall. It cascaded and splashed down many white steps, getting wider and wider, even reaching 150 feet Frank thought, then it frothed and flowed into the Grand Basin. There were also two

FESTIVAL HALL AND CENTRAL CASCADES.

No description can convey to the mind an adequate idea of the beauty of this wonderful architectural masterpiece designed by Cass Gilbert, of New York. Notwithstanding the great size of the building the festive effect is shown in every part. The building is 200 feet in diameter and 200 feet high. The auditorium contains seats for 3,500 and a stage large enough for the great choruses of hundreds of voices which appear from time to time in the musical programs of the Exposition. The largest pipe organ in the world is a part of the equipment. Mr. Gilbert is the designer of the exterior of the building alone. The beautiful setting of cascades and sculpture, the massive colonnades, fifty feet high, and the interior architecture of the building were all done by the chief of design of the Exposition, Mr. E. L. Masqueray, of New York. The great beauty as well as the massive character of this centerpiece of the World's Fair will be long remembered by visitors. To those who have not seen it, this picture must convey a lasting impression. One may gain some idea of the vastness of this feature by noting the tiny stature of the people appearing in the photograph.

## LARGEST PIPE ORGAN IN THE WORLD.

The development of the pipe organ reached its highest stage in the magnificent instrument installed in Festival Hall. It is really five organs in one and all five organs can be played by one performer by means of connecting attachments. The arrangement draws out the tremendous power and beauty of the entire five organs, a feat otherwise utterly beyond the range of human fingers. The player sits at a movable console or key desk and his fingers must command five manuals or keyboards, making a flight of five stairs. The key desk is movable, being connected with the organ by 150 feet of electric cable. The player must command not only the five rows of keys but 140 draw-stop knobs, 36 couple draws, 46 push buttons belonging to the adjustable combination system, and all of the feet levers controlling the expressive powers of the whole organ. The organ contains 10,159 pipes and 1,300 magnets. Five thousand open circuits connect the various parts and two ten-horse power motors are used to pump the bellows and operate the organ. This great instrument is used in the concerts of Festival Hall throughout the Exposition.

Fountains in front of Festival Hall

Grand Basin from Festival Hall and the Cascades

COLONNADE OF STATES, EASTERN ARM.

The Colonnade of States, stretching east and west from Festival Hall, is a part of the great architectural and landscape composition that crowns the ridge of Art Hill. In each of the hemicycles in the great sweep of the arms is placed a heroic figure symbolic of the state or territory it represents. Here are brought together the idealizations of the fourteen commonwealths of the Louisiana Purchase. The seven in the eastern arm are Missouri (1821), Iowa (1846), Kansas (1861), Colorado (1876), South Dakota (1889), Wyoming (l890) and Oklahoma (1890). The view is from a point near Festival Hall, At the east extreme of this arm of the Colonnade stands one of the superb restaurant pavilions, and at the left of the picture is seen a bit of the beautiful roof of the Palace of Mines and Metallurgy, serving as a background for the basin of the east cascade, which is surmounted by the gilded figure of the Spirit of the Pacific. The wonderful Cascade Gardens spread their glories around and about the scene. From any of the seats along the Colonnade a satisfying view may be had of the whole of the central group of palaces, with the waterways, the gardens and the sculpture that make the picture a delight.

Pristine white bridge over a lagoon.

smaller cascades, one on either side of the larger. The Grand Basin was a huge man-made lake which extended the length of four majestic buildings, two on each side of it. Many boats on the water were carrying passengers to and from all parts of the fair, often taking little detours into the lagoons and under the white pristine bridges. Fountains sprayed into the air, making mini-rainbows in the sunlight.

Surrounding Festival Hall, near the steps, were numerous statues of smiling children astride the backs of fishes, creations of mothers cuddling babies, a sculpture of a bison and an Indian—such magic—the brothers could not believe the magnificence of it all.

Rudy continued to be enthralled with what he saw. "Oh, Frank, did you ever see anything like this? Look at the sparkling water and the way it ripples in the breeze. And the boats! There are so many different kinds."

The boys had gone down the steps from Festival Hall and were strolling along the walkway. Frank pointed toward the water. "I think those in front are Venetian boats from Italy, Rudy, gondolas. I've seen pictures of them in my geography book. It states in our booklet that the men pushing the boats are gondoliers and they often sing for their passengers."

They noticed other boats on the basin: little swan-shaped ones, electric launches with red or green striped top canvas to keep the sun out; some others were shaped like dragons, and one or two were festooned with vines, wreathes and flowers. They were all filled with people—laughing, singing, and having a wonderful time.

Frank didn't want to rush Rudy, but he was eager to find the Palace of Agriculture where he would see his father's exhibit. They decided to do some walking, though there were many ways one could travel. The fair boasted an intramural railway, zebu-drawn carts, wagons, burros, Oriental jinrickshas, roller chairs pushed by attendants, touring cars, camels, and always the boats.

To their right and left were huge palaces. Their booklet said these were called by various names, depending on the exhibits. There was the Palace of Transportation, the Palace of Education, the Palace of Industry and on and on. The fair covered 1240 acres—large enough to be a town of its own. It was so vast, they could not see the end of it.

They strolled across the white arched bridges which spanned the side lagoons. Rudy would stop at the top of a bridge and watch whatever boat was coming as it glided beneath him, so Frank watched too. He noticed that some of the ladies in the boats were carrying ruffled parasols to keep the sun off their faces. It had been warm all fall. As he was watching with Rudy, he saw a dark-haired girl close her fancy parasol, just as her boat floated to the bridge where the brothers were standing. She looked up and smiled at Frank. Frank smiled back and tipped his black bowler hat. His eyes followed the girl as the boat went on down the lagoon in the sunshine. Rudy walked away with his hands in his pockets, grinning.

GROUP OF GONDOLAS ON GRAND BASIN.

The beatiful Venetian craft that ply the waters of the Exposition lagoons give just the needed touch of romance. A gondola anywhere is a luxurious and a useful boat, but it Is never prosaic. Many of these long, dark, graceful boats are in constant use at the Fair, and they form charming pictures as the swarthy oarsmen propel them with easy grace, standing at the prow and stern, facing forward. These are real gondoliers from Venice, many of them gifted singers, and the lagoons ring with music as the evening falls and the lights come forth. Often the pedestrian passing over a bridge is almost startled at the sound of music, and looking over the rail he sees a gondola gliding softly beneath him, the rowers intoning liquid Italian words; or perhaps the party of visitors is in the mood for song and is sending forth a joyous chorus. The view shown is the west portion of the Grand Basin, with one of the restaurant pavilions rising in the center, above the cascades. Two of the beautiful fountains are throwing their cooling spray high in air, and half-a-dozen gondolas are lying at rest.   Nowhere else except in Venice can such a scene be found, and even there the setting cannot equal this.

CARNIVAL SCENE ON GRAND BASIN.

The view given above shows a part of a water pageant crossing the Grand Basin. This basin is a broad expanse of water lying between the Palaces of Electricity and Education and directly in front of the cascades. The point of view is near the Louisiana Purchase Monument. The Grand Basin is a part of the lagoon system, the lagoon to the right encircling the Palace of Electricity, and the one to the left surrounding the Palace of Education. Upon these lagoons is a great variety of craft including gondolas brought from Venice, peacock boats, swan boats, dragon boats and handsome electric launches. The trip is one of the romantic experiences of the visitor. Upon the gala occasions which the picture illustrates, the boats are decked out in flowers, plants, flags and banners, and a procession thus organized makes a very beautiful scene. At night colored lights serve for purposes of decoration. The lagoons are in the heart of the Exposition and from the boats one may view the glorious central picture with unusual satisfaction and pleasure.

Festival of Boats on Grand Basin

Touring Car on the Fair Grounds

TRANSPORTATION AT THE FAIR—ELECTRIC LAUNCH AND GONDOLA.

In the decorative scheme of the World's Fair, water plays an important part. The lagoons, encircling two of the most beautiful buildings, form a continuous water-way a mile and a half in length, and the Grand Basin is a broad, beautiful lake, a quivering mirror of stately columns and dappled sky. At the foot of Cascade Hill the surface is broken by four geysers the central jets of which send a stream of water a hundred feet high that breaks into a shower of mist as it descends. There are hut two ways of seeing the central cascade and enjoying the geyser spray. The conveyances are electric launches and gondolas; the latter were brought from Venice and the gondoliers came with them. As the swarthy Italians stand on the stern of the graceful crafts, dipping the long slender oar to the measure of some southern love song, the sight is a most charming one. This sight can be enjoyed best from a seat in one of the delightful launches. The launch holds thirty passengers and the fare is a quarter of a dollar. The gondola fee is double that sum, and the boat accommodates but twelve. At frequent intervals the lagoon is spanned by artistic bridges the under surface of which forms an excellent sounding-board for the singer.

A Boat like the one Grace was in when Frank saw her.

## TRANSPORTATION AT THE FAIR—THE AUTOMOBILE.

The first means of locomotion that greets the new-comer at any of the prominent entrances to the World's Fair is the great lumbering automobile, the best type of storage battery motor carriage now in use. This is the machine that, in all probability, will occupy a place at the great International Exposition of 1950, in the historic automobile exhibit, alongside of the 1830 pattern of steam engines, to show the crude beginning of a great invention. Clumsy as the motor car of today is, yet it is a valuable means of transportation, and especially valuable to the visitor on his first day at the Fair. Each machine is operated by a chauffeur who is a living guide-book and who takes delight in giving of his store of information. The ride is four miles in length, around all the great exhibit palaces, through the foreign section, past the most beautiful floral displays and around the Grand Basin. The guide points out. one after another, the buildings, statues and gardens, and has many amusing and interesting things to tell about the specially important or novel exhibits inside the buildings. A visit to the Exposition could not begin more profitably than by a tour on the automobile.

"It may be difficult getting you home, Frank," Rudy teased.

They found the Palace of Agriculture on their map. The building covered twenty-three acres, and the nave, or center of it, was to show the large figure displays of corn, cotton, rice, tobacco, and sugar. Pa's corn would be displayed in the Missouri structure. Many states had areas of their own to show off prize things they could grow.

Rudy was eager to see more of the fair. "Come on, Frank. I saw the biggest wheel in the distance that I've even seen. It must be the one built by Mr. Ferris— the wheel that came from the earlier Chicago World's Fair of 1893. The information says it can carry 2000 people on just one trip. How could that be true?"

"Why don't you go and find out, Rudy. Take the railway and get off at number nine. I'll meet you in about an hour at the ferris wheel. You wait for me there. I want to locate the Missouri section first."

Rudy noticed that the railway was different from the trolley. The trolley had steps leading to it. The railway could not be entered unless the train had stopped at a platform, and then one just walked into the car.

Rudy exited the train-car and raced toward the wheel. The closer he got the more he realized the size of it. It went 250 feet into the air, making it easy to see all over the fair and beyond. There were thirty-six cars that could hold sixty people in each car, and every car had its own attendant. The wheel contained 4200 tons of steel, the axel 70 tons alone, and it rotated four times per hour.

Rudy's head was tilted back and up as he gaped. Just then Frank walked up behind him. "I decided to come with you, Rudy. I will go to the Agricultural Palace later."

Rudy was a little surprised. "How did you get here so fast?"

"I took one of those zebu-drawn carts—it was coming right to the wheel. The animal that pulled it was sure strong. But it looked like a cow. No, I just decided it would be better if we stayed together."

Rudy was still staring at the wheel. "It looks like a big wagon wheel, except it could only be used by a giant. Come on, let's hurry and get in line."

Frank's stomach did a little dive as they were pulled into the sky. There wasn't much motion after that, so he relaxed and enjoyed the view. Some windows were open a little and the air was wonderful. They could see where they came through the gate, the flowing cascades, the basin, and just below them, Japanese gardens and a teahouse. Frank had read that some of the bonsai trees that Japan was exhibiting were 200 years old.

Everyone around them was chattering about the fair. Someone pointed out the Jerusalem Dome, another spoke of seeing live babies in incubators; a well-dressed man was praising the St. Louis Restaurant on the Pike, and there was mention of Patagonian Indians seven feet tall. Another talked of a ride on the Pike that took one through hell. Most of it the brothers didn't even understand.

## PALACE OF AGRICULTURE

Covered 21 acres

TRANSPORTATION AT THE FAIR—INTRAMURAL RAILROAD.

The enormous area of the Exposition grounds is to some extent obliterated by the excellent intramural service. The cars are large and commodious, the very perfection of city street cars, which they resemble in all respects but one. They have no steps leading down from the front and rear platforms. The place of the steps is supplied by station platforms that are on a level with the floor of the car. Stops are made for passengers only at these stations, which are so located as to minimize the walking of the visitor who is bound for any important exhibit in the remote part of the grounds. The Intramural road is a double-track electric line, largely on the level ground. In some places it passes through deep cuts that are almost tunnels and again it is virtually an elevated road, running over large stretches of trestle. The stations are numbered from 1 to 17, beginning at the west side and ending at the east side of the Plaza of St. Louis. The ride, for which the charge is ten cents, is seven miles long, and the stations, after one has passed the heart of the Exposition, are close to the Administration building, the Stadium, the Model Indian School and the outside Anthropological exhibit, the Philippines, the Agricultural group, the Art Galleries, the Plateau of the States and the Government Pavilion.

TRANSPORTATION AT THE FAIR.

ZEBU RACING CART.　　　　　　　TRAINED ELEPHANT.

Among the many attractions of the great trained animal circus none is more interesting or amusing to the children than a ride in the zebu cart. The zebu, more commonly known as the sacred ox, is an animal possessing the best qualities of the horse and the cow. Its harness is exceedingly simple, consisting of a yoke and a ring through the nose, to which the lines are attached. In India the zebu is bred for racing purposes; but the races are a part of the most sacred religious ceremonies, and the Hindoo members of the circus refuse to participate in the races at the World's Fair, considering such use of the zebu as sacrilege of the worst form.

Another amusement that appeals especially to the little girls is riding on the back of one of the many Hagenbeck elephants. In the Orient the elephant and the camel are the chief beasts of burden, and of the two the elephant is much the easier to ride. His gait is more steady, and the Indian howdah or elephant saddle resembles a great easy chair rather than a saddle. The majority of the elephants that perform such marvelous tricks and are such docile carriers of timid little maidens, were absolutely wild and untrained when the World's Fair opened. Yet they are the most teachable of all animals, yielding to training more readily even than does the dog or the horse.

THE OBSERVATION WHEEL.

Perhaps the best start that the Exposition sightseer can make is to make the trip in the great wheel which first appeared at the Columbian Exposition as the Ferris Wheel. It is located near the center of the grounds and is easily found, though it is much less conspicuous than it was at Chicago. It looked immense at Chicago; in St. Louis it merely looks large. Yet it carries the visitor steadily and safely to a height of about 250 feet and gives him a constantly shifting view of everything, great and small, within the Exposition grounds, not to mention the leagues of town and country added to the prospect. When one has had this bird's-eye view, he goes about the grounds with a sense of familiarity with his surroundings that no map can give. The construction of the wheel presented great engineering difficulties. It contains 4,200 tons of metal, the axle alone weighing 70 tons, and this mass is formed into what may be called a bicycle wheel, with tension spokes. It bears thirty-six roomy cars, each in charge of an attendant. It is no uncommon occurrence to seethe wheel carrying 1,500 or 2,000 persons, making four revolutions in an hour. The ride is comfortable and moreover it is safe. More than 3,000,000 people have been carried without injury, and those who have been in the cars in violent storms aver that there was no discomfort.

North Side: George Ferris

266 Feet in Air:

The Ferris Wheel Turns and Mrs. Ferris Gives a Toast:

Her Husband's Health and the Wheel's Success--

Two Carloads of More or Less Nervous Guests Join Her in Drinking It.

The builder of the first ferris wheel. The one at the Fair was originally built for the Chicago Exposition of 1893, then it was later moved to St. Louis.

JAPANESE GARDENS AND TEA-HOUSES.

The Japanese at home are not given to erecting large, isolated buildings, but incline to collections of smaller and more varied structures than do Americans and Europeans. The national exhibit of Japan at the Fair is therefore in keeping with the spirit and taste of the people. The large hillside area which is occupied by Japan lies east of the Observation wheel and southwest of the Palace of Machinery. Dainty gardens, with winding paths and green sward make the spot a pleasant one in which to enjoy the smiling hospitality of the Orientals. There are cascades and fountains, and plashing little streams spanned by quaint bridges or crossed by lines of stepping-stones. There are pretty pagodas, beds of flowering plants, and rock-work ornamented by giant cranes. Many interesting buildings are within the enclosure. In one of them Japanese artists may be seen at their work, and in another, extensive collections of Japanese wares are offered for sale. The beautiful pavilion shown in the engraving is used as a tea-house, and is modeled after the Kikakuji Palace still standing at Kioto after 480 years of service. In the upper rooms are models of Japanese idols and images, and on the first floor one stops to take tea, whether he cares for it or not, just for the pleasure of being served by the dainty and charming maidens whose English is as limited as it is delightful.

95

After the ferris wheel ride, they decided to return to the St. Louis Plaza, which was at the end of the basin, to see some of the statues and exhibits. Frank was interested in the Palace of Transportation because it housed a large locomotive on a turntable. The train's main headlight stayed on continually, lighting all parts of the arena. There were other displays he had already read about. He would look for some of the 122 automobiles that had been in the Parade of Automobiles earlier in the year.

Rudy wanted to find the log cabin of General Ulysses S. Grant, leader of the North in the Civil War. Pa always said slavery was wrong, and the General must have been a great man who fought for what he believed in. He had lived in Missouri and built the cabin only eleven years before entering the war. Also displayed at the fair was the railroad car that Abraham Lincoln had traveled in.

"I'm tired, Frank, but I don't want to miss any part of the fair. It is getting difficult to walk—there are so many people here." They had already visited other places before they arrived at their destination.

They ambled around until they saw the tall monument they were seeking. "Rudy, this is the Monument of Peace dedicated to the Louisiana Purchase Centennial. It has been 100 years since France sold all the land between the Mississippi River and the Rocky Mountains to the United States. That opened a path for people to live here, or to travel on to the Pacific Ocean.

GIANT INDIANS FROM PATAGONIA.

In collecting the ethnology exhibit of living races the most remote parts of the world have been drawn upon. In this congress of the races are included a family of Tehuelche Indians from Patagonia, remarkable for their powerful frames and commanding height. They are a peaceable people and have many noble traits. The children are taught to ride horseback even before they learn to walk. At the World's Fair they live in a house of the same character that they have in their native country. In fact one of the principal features of the Ethnology exhibit is to show not only the primitive people but their habitations also. The hut of the Patagonian Giants contains but two rooms and is entirely covered with horsehide. These Indians are said to be rapidly disappearing on account of the inroads of civilization, Patagonia being a part of the Argentine Republic. They are employed as herders, and carry on a few primitive industries.

PALACE OF TRANSPORTATION.

The visitor is reminded of a great railroad station as he notes the architecture of the Palace of Transportation, which stands west of the Palace of Varied Indusries and north of the Palace of Machinery, The building is 525 feet by 1,300 feet, covering fifteen acres. Beneath the expansive roof are displayed all the modem methods of transportation together with historical exhibits of great interest. The historical display of old locomotives shows graphically the long struggle from the time of the stage coach to the era of the modern palace car. Visitors are permitted to inspect the most palatial trains. A huge locomotive stands in the center of the building upon a turn-table. In the western end of the building is a laboratory for testing the efficiency of locomotives. The old horse car and the modern trolley car stand side by side. The display of automobiles shows the remarkable possibilities of this new means of travel. Motor boats and other water craft are here in goodly numbers while the road vehicles for all sorts of purposes are not forgotten. Models of railway stations, cars and other railway equipment are displayed.

## THE WORLD'S FAIR AUTOMOBILE RUN—ARRIVAL OF NEW YORK CARS IN ST. LOUIS AFTER A RUN OF 1300 MILES

The New York contingent of automobilists which left for St. Louis on July 24 reached its destination on August 10. The first of the tourists to arrive was Mr. W. C. Hurlburt, who was officially reported in East St. Louis at 1.15 on the afternoon of that date. The last day's run was made under trying conditions, the stretch of road between Mount Olive and East St. Louis having been made almost impassable by heavy rains. Of the seventy-nine machines which started on the tour, only four failed to finish at St. Louis

GENERAL GRANT'S LOG CABIN.

It was a happy thought to bring to the World's Fair such a potent reminder of one of America's greatest generals as a cabin built by his own hands. This structure stands in the wooded part of the Exposition grounds, a few rods east of the art palaces. The cabin of logs was built by General Ulysses S. Grant when he was a frontiersman and farmer in St. Louis County in 1854, only eleven years before he achieved the great victory at Appomattox that made his name immortal. The cabin was carefully taken down, removed from its original site and rebuilt upon the Exposition grounds exactly as it stood originally. At the dedication of the Exposition, General Frederick D. Grant took the opportunity to visit the cabin built by his illustrious father and evinced much interest in its preservation. The cabin teaches a great lesson to American youth, showing that humble tasks cannot demean the manly or the truly great.

A MODERN TURNTABLE IN THE TRANSPORTATION PALACE.

Centrally located in the Palace of Transportation is the working exhibit of the C., C., C. & St. L. Railway (Big Four Route), a monster locomotive and tender mounted on a turntable resembling an inverted bridge-truss, the whole assemblage of parts revolving easily on a relatively small horizontal circle of steel, so that the headlight, carried high in air, illuminates in turn every corner of the great building. As the turntable, with its well-poised burden, revolves in its 75-foot circle, the 79-inch driving-wheels rotate rapidly. Electric power is used for moving all of the mechanism, and only the result is seen. The American Locomotive Company built the engine, and the Chicago Bridge and Iron Works supplied the turntable. In the circle of floor-space below the sweep of the turntable, the railroad company has laid out a map showing the route traversed by its lines. Besides its own weight, the great turntable carries that of the locomotive, 184,000 pounds, and the tender, 140,000 pounds—162 tons in all. To balance the greater weight of the engine and give steadiness to the motion, 55,000 pounds of sand are carried in the tender. Engines of this type haul ten cars at a rate of sixty miles an hour.

PRIVATE RAILWAY COACH USED BY ABRAHAM LINCOLN.

This quaint piece of transportation equipment is valued more for its historic worth than as a relic of pioneer railroading, because of its association with Abraham Lincoln, whose private car it was during the stirring period of the Civil War. Instead of having a place among other rolling stock in the Palace of Transportation, the old car is therefore housed in the Lincoln Museum with other relics of the martyred president, including the log cabin in which Lincoln was born. The coach represents the highest type of the railroad palace car of forty years ago and is interesting as a comparison with the modern Pullman. Its interior is furnished in the richest of tapestries, mirrors and upholstering, but these have become worn with age and, like the woodwork, have fallen into decay. It was from the platform of this car that Lincoln greeted the people in his travels during his second campaign for the Presidency, and in the parlor of the car he entertained many of the famous men of his time. The coach was constructed by the government in the workshop at Alexandria, Va., and made its first trips over the Pennsylvania and Baltimore & Ohio lines.

LOUISIANA PURCHASE MONUMENT AND PALACE OF VARIED INDUSTRIES.

The Plaza of St. Louis, in which the Louisiana Purchase Monument stands, is a favorite gathering place for World's Fair visitors. The monument, designed by E. L. Masqueray, is one of the most artistic ornaments of the Exposition. The crowning figure of Peace is by Karl Bitter. At the base is another sculptured group by Mr. Bitter commemorating the signing of the Louisiana Purchase Treaty. In this group appear the figures of Marbois, the representative of Napoleon, the first Consul of France; Robert R. Livingston, United States Minister to France, and James Monroe, afterward President, the special envoy of President Jefferson, sent to assist Livingston in the negotiations. From the Plaza of St. Louis the visitor may see Festival Hall, the Cascade Gardens and other beautiful features.

LIBERTY BELL, PENNSYLVANIA BUILDING.

The Liberty Bell is exhibited for the first time west of the Mississippi River at the World's Fair. Upon the occasion of its arrival in St. Louis the school children of the city-turned out by tens of thousands to receive the precious memento. The bell is in the rotunda of the Pennsylvania building and is the shrine of patriotic Americans who visit the Exposition. The bell was cast a quarter of a century before it called the colonists to the first public reading of the Declaration of Independence, but it bore a prophetic inscription from the first day of its existence, from Leviticus, xxv: 10, "Proclaim liberty throughout all the land and unto all the inhabitants thereof." The bell weighs 2,080 pounds, is four feet in diameter at the lip and three feet high. The familiar crack in the bell occurred while it was being tolled for the funeral of Chief Justice John Marshall, July 8, 1835. The bell was cast in London in 1752 after the mold of "the Great Tom of Westminster." A month after it was hung in the state house at Philadelphia it was cracked and was re-cast on the same mold and with the same inscription by an American firm.

PALACE OF VARIED INDUSTRIES.

The long colonnades, domes and towers are the distinguishing features in the architecture of the Palace of Varied Industries. It has the same dimensions as the Palace of Manufactures, being 525 feet wide by 1,200 feet in length and covering an area of fourteen acres. The exhibits within this beautiful palace are gathered from many states and countries. Germany and Japan are rivals in the extent of space covered, but their rivalry ends there, for the exhibits are radically different. Germany occupies a large area in the northeastern corner, the installation for which is very elaborate. The manufacturers of fine wares have put forth their best efforts with results most creditable and interesting. In this building the exhibits are those of art industries, such as art pottery, cut glass and art glass, office and household furniture, brushes, fine leather articles, jewelry, silversmiths' and goldsmiths' wares, clocks and watches, products in marble, bronze, cast iron, wrought iron, paper hangings and upholsterers' decorations. The Japan exhibit occupies a very large space in the southwestern corner with a beautiful temple as its entrance.

"I learned that too, Frank. Miss Agnes, my teacher, said the Louisiana Treaty was second in importance only to the Declaration of Independence. Say, did you know the Liberty Bell is here on display also? I just have to see that."

"Yes, Rudy, and there are statues here of Lewis and Clark, Joliet, and de Soto. If it hadn't been for the explorers of that time, our grandfather would not have been able to settle in Missouri. It would have belonged to France." Frank grinned and added, "We would have been saying, 'Oui, Oui', instead of 'Yes, Yes'. Little wonder they decided to send the Liberty Bell, crack and all." Frank loved to say these things because Rudy always laughed.

"Frank, there is another statue, honoring the families that traveled in covered wagons, like Pa did. Can you imagine the hardships those people endured to get us here?" Rudy looked at the statue in awe. He decided it was almost too much to comprehend.

It had been a long rewarding day. They still hadn't gotten to the Palace of Agriculture, but there was always tomorrow. Dusk was turning to dark now, and suddenly the ivory buildings became a glow of festive lights. As the lights came on, they heard a breath-taking exclamation all over the fairgrounds. There wasn't one electric light at their house, and here they were seeing millions of them. It said in their brochure that Thomas Edison, the inventor, had overseen the implementation of all the electric lights on the fair's buildings.

Music wafted across the basin as the Italian singers sang their songs, and some people joined in. "Frank, let's just sit here on this bench by the water and listen. Will there ever be another time like this in our lives?" Light from the buildings danced on the water, and soft music continued to drift over the entire scene.

Frank could not answer. He knew Rudy was right. He knew he was witnessing something that millions of people were hopeful to see now or in the future. But they would not and could not. It would all be over. In a few weeks, the buildings would be torn down, and it would all be history.

Frank felt very grateful for his father's efforts and foresight. He was also humbled by his brother's hospitality and Francine's caring. What if they had never had a chance to see the fair—this knowledge, this peace and serenity? It all came about because thousands of people here and abroad had an interest in human welfare. It touched him to know his Pa was one of them.

Rudy studied the changing colors of the Cascades and then said quietly, "Frank, I have a great idea!"

"Here we go again," teased Frank.

"No, really—I think we should convince Francine to come to the fair with us tomorrow. We could visit lots of areas and one of them an amusement area called the Pike. Do you think she would like that?"

"We'll ask her when we get home. We must go now; they are expecting us for a late supper."

PALACE OF LIBERAL ARTS AT NIGHT.

PALACES OF MACHINERY AND ELECTRICITY AT NIGHT.

PALACE OF ELECTRICITY AT NIGHT.

The beautiful Palace of Electricity is one of the central structures of the Exposition, standing opposite the Palace of Education on the west side of the Grand Basin, The Lagoon system extends entirely around the building and the approach is by means of several ornamental bridges. The entire setting is most beautiful. The Palace of Varied Industries stands on the north, the Palace of Machinery on the west and the Cascade Gardens rise on the south. The building covers eight acres and is one of the most costly on account of the many lofty columns and entablatures, the high towers at corners and entrances and the liberal use of sculpture. The architecture is such as to make a picture of unusual beauty when the electric current is turned on and the thousands of bulbs glow with festive radiance. In the brilliant night picture the statuary on the lofty corner towers and elsewhere stands out prominently against the dark sky. The sculpture on the corners is by Bela L. Pratt. The standing figure represents Light, while at her feet crouch in the shadow of their mantles, figures representing Darkness.

109

PALACE OF EDUCATION AT NIGHT.

The Exposition of 1904 is cosmopolitan, it is universal, it is ancient and it is modern. No one need try to enjoy what another enjoys. There is variety enough to give everyone full sway for his pleasure or whim. In the Palace of Education we have a triumph of classic architecture, transformed at night and made visible by the latest achievements in electrical engineering. By day one thinks of this building as a stately ivory structure housing innumerable exhibits that show the latest supreme effort of the great minds of the age. When one sees it at night, he forgets that it has even so remotely utilitarian a phase. Seen across the Grand Basin, in one of the most prominent situations on the grounds, the Palace of Education is simply part of a glorious picture. It stands on a great island that came into being when the lagoons were carved out, and it faces an expanse of water whose beauties are enhanced a hundred fold by the sparkle and reflection of myriads of lights. The outlines of the building are reduplicated in the mirror of the Grand Basin, where they sway and flutter and palpitate as the lake is agitated by the increasing flow from the cascades and fountains, or seamed and rippled by the gondoliers' oars. The Exposition should be seen by day and by night.    If but one visit can be made, let that be at night.

PALACES OF ELECTRICITY AND VARIED INDUSTRIES AT NICHT.

# DINNER AND MORE SURPRISES

Francine cooked a meal that most farm people only dream about. Frank especially was very appreciative. She served five courses and with great ease, causing her guests to feel it had been no trouble at all. Her table was set with pink linens, gleaming silver and a milk glass vase filled with red zinnias and pink mums. It all matched the décor in her home.

The soup was Francine's special recipe for chicken gumbo, followed by a crisp lettuce, tomato, and red onion salad with a cheesy, garlic dressing. Frank kept asking her how she made the gumbo, and she volunteered that he could have the recipe.

Lime sorbet and white grapes was the next course, very French and quite delicious. Their hostess said that the course that followed the soup and salad was to cleanse the palate so that the main entree could be enjoyed more fully. After Rudy tasted it, he thought it was like ice cream, but he didn't say so. He did say it was good.

There were lot's of m-m-m-m's when Francine brought the tender beef steaks to the table, along with a mounded dish of buttery mashed potatoes. And for dessert, she had made homemade ice cream and her favorite chocolate cupcakes, rocky mountains. When Rudy bit into the marshmallow coated cupcake, he found some melted carmel. Before Frank even asked, Francine said he could have that recipe too. It was a supper they would never forget.

Fred was mighty pleased with the efforts Francine had made for his brothers, and he told her so. The brothers readily agreed, continuing to compliment her on the meal. Then Francine invited them to have coffee in the parlor.

After they had settled themselves on the red velvet chairs and Francine had passed some crispy cookies, Fred walked to a desk and reached under it. He pulled out a violin case and handed it to Rudy.

"Can you play this for us, Rudy?" Fred asked.

Rudy opened the case and took out the violin. His eyes shone as he held the instrument. He loved music and had been quite excited about the ragtime tunes he'd heard floating about the fair. He raised the violin to his chin and played "Over the Waves". It was the only song he knew. Everyone clapped and Rudy blushed a bit.

Fred smiled and said, "Rudy would you like to have that violin?" During the conversation at the table, Frank had been telling Fred about some of Rudy's talents, which had given Fred the idea.

Rudy was almost speechless. He breathed a soft "yes, I would Fred, and thank you" and held the violin like it was a newborn baby. Fred could see he had given the violin to the right person.

They continued to visit about their lives on the farm and Fred's job. All of them asked each other so many questions, and it was soon decided that Fred and

Francine must come to the farm for a visit. Francine offered them more coffee, then Frank cleared his throat to ask her about the next day.

"Francine, Rudy and I decided that you should accompany us tomorrow to the fair. Would you do us the honor of going with us?"

Rudy thought Frank's request very gallant, and he was ready to pursue it. "Oh, Yes, Francine. Do come with us. We have not been to the Agricultural Building yet or the Pike. The Pike is a place of entertainment we're told, and if it might be something to your liking, we'd love to have you with us."

Francine seemed pleased to be asked. She told them she had not yet attended the fair, but wanted to. It seemed Fred's work had kept them from going, and she didn't wish to go alone—no lady ever did that. She ended her reply with a gracious acceptance.

The next morning found them up early, looking forward to the day. Francine dressed in a long, pearl-gray organdy that had a white and gray hat and parasol to match. It was a little late in the fall for anything white, but the weather had been unseasonably warm so she decided to wear it. Frank thought her outfit was beautiful and the parasol much like the young lady's that he had seen in the boat, when she went under the bridge.

Francine's dress was full and flowing, and the brothers would often be needed to assist her up and down steps and in and out of places. Rudy and

Frank had donned new shirts, polished their shoes, and set their bowler hats at a rakish angle. They were off to the fair.

On the way there, the brothers asked many questions about life in the big city. Francine began to realize this was an education in itself for them. When they finally entered the fair, the brothers grinned and watched Francine's face. Even this elite St. Louis lady was impressed by what she saw. Her mouth made little o's as she viewed the monuments, the white buildings, and on to the lovely steps with its waterfalls and spraying fountains. She was as overwhelmed as they had been the day before. The brothers led her to the Colonnades, Festival Hall, and the Cascades. It was wonderful to view them again, but it was more fun to watch Francine's appreciation.

After they had seen most of that area, Francine said, "Frank, there are only two other things I'd like to see before we go on to the Pike." She saw that the brothers were listening attentively so she continued. "I want to visit the Flower Clock, and I wish to see the Sunken Gardens."

Frank knew in his heart that if his Ma were there, she would have made the same requests. He looked at his map, locating the areas of Francine's choice. About that time, some attendants came by with available roller chairs. Frank stopped three of them and told Francine and Rudy to each get in one. Francine started to protest, but Frank was adamant and said they would soon get tired

## FESTIVAL HALL AND GRAND BASIN.

The view shown is one of the majestic sweeps of the Cascade Gardens and their settings. At the left rises the dome of Festival Hall, 200 feet above the crown of the hill on which it stands. Rich carpets of sward slope gracefully down toward the waters of the Grand Basin, and the wonderful rainbow gardening makes a picture not to be excelled elsewhere. The observer contemplating this scene faces nearly west. The western arm of the Colonnade of States connects Festival Hall with the restaurant pavilion near the center of the picture. The ever-charming cascade at the west shows clearly, though the great central cascade can be better seen from the Grand Basin. Toward the right, the 250-foot circle of the Observation Wheel is sharply defined against the sky, and at the extreme right a portion of the Palace of Machinery may be seen. A part of the white walls of Jerusalem peers over the hill. The scene is one of majesty, of vastness, of many objects combined into a satisfying and harmonious whole. It fills the eye, and delights with a wealth of color and grace of line, and charms with the swirl and play of water. The surface of the basin ripples and dapples under the wind and the sun, and to complete the satisfaction of the beholder the sounds of music and of voices add the human note.

enough. They all three enjoyed being pushed to the fair's railway stop while the sons watched the crowds and Francine the fashions.

The Flower Clock was magnificent. It was 112 feet in diameter, right in front of the Agricultural Palace. It consisted of many varieties of colorful fall blooms. All during the fair, different flowers had been planted there. Each hand of the operating clock weighed 2500 pounds, and the minute hand was 75 feet long. It moved five feet every minute. It was controlled by a master clock and moved by an air-compressor. The hourly numbers were in different kinds and colors of plants. Francine exclaimed more than once how beautiful it was. Then she motioned toward the Palace of Agriculture, but the brothers had already decided to go there the next day.

Later, they arrived at the Sunken Gardens. Francine insisted on walking in the center, closer to the blooms, and Frank and Rudy strolled with her. The flowers had been planted to look like a tapestry, woven in many brilliant, seasonal colors. And surrounding the area, which was lower than the walkways above, were numerous iron benches for people to rest and enjoy the scene. Frank and Rudy liked the gardens too. The benches looked inviting, and they decided to sit and rest awhile.

"Do either of you know where St. Louis acquired it's name?" Francine asked, settling her dress about her and lowering her white and gray satin parasol.

The brothers shook their heads. They had never given much thought as to how places were named. They politely asked Francine to tell them.

"There was a king of France, titled Louis the Ninth," she began. "The nine is always written in Roman numerals—like this IX." She used a pencil and showed them on one margin of her map. "Some years later, King Louis was canonized—that means they made him a Saint because they believed he loved his people and because of his crusades. The founder of St. Louis, Mr. Laclede, then named our city after the king."

Rudy was listening intently. "I wonder who Kidder is named after?" he questioned.

"Probably no one, Rudy," Frank replied. Then he said grinning, "Not every town was named after a person—at least I hope not. What about 'Tightwad' or 'Cross Timbers'? Those are both towns in Missouri too."

They were laughing together as Francine arose from the bench, opened her parasol and said, "Now, I would like to experience a wagon ride to the Pike. I am taking you both to lunch at the St. Louis Restaurant which is located there. I understand it is one of President Theodore Roosevelt's favorite eating places. Would this plan be acceptable?"

Eagerly the brothers helped her on to the wagon, being very careful of her dress, then climbed on themselves. The driver whistled to his team, all the while humming a tune he'd heard at the fair. Francine opened her parasol and smiled at their fellow passengers.

"Gee, this is just like being back on the farm," Rudy said, laughing.

"What a wonderful time we are having!" voiced Frank.

## THE FLORAL CLOCK.

This is one of the novelties of the Exposition. The great dial, 112 feet in diameter, is laid out in flowers and plants of bright foliage, and is located just north of the Palace or Agriculture, on the slope of a hill, hence it is visible from many points and from great distances. Each of the hands weighs 2,500 pounds. The minute hand is 74 feet long, and it moves five feet every minute. The five-minute spaces between the hour-marks are clearly marked off by differences in color into minute-spaces each five feet long. Unlike other clocks, this one moves rapidly for a few seconds and then stops on a mark. This is repeated every minute. When one goes up the hill and looks at the beautiful machinery that actuates this clock, he understands why it moves in this manner. There is a master clock under glass, and at the beginning of each minute it sets in motion a compressed-air piston that moves the mighty hands. Hours and half-hours are struck on a bell weighing 5,000 pounds. Close at hand there is a terrestrial globe, revolving once in twenty-four hours, on which one may read the time of day or night at any place on earth. There is also an hour-glass, holding 100 pounds of sand, reversed at the end of each hour. Everything connected with the interesting exhibit is moved by compressed air, but it is all controlled by the delicate, accurate master clock.

TRANSPORTATION AT THE FAIR—THE ROLLER CHAIR.

For the visitor who wishes to rest and at the same time see the splendid pictures of the World's Fair there are many facilities for locomotion, such as the Intramural railroad, the launches and gondolas, the burros and little electric road through the Mining Gulch. For him who must rest, and yet has no time to lose from the exhibits within the buildings, but one means of transportation is provided. There is need of but one. This is the roller chair. The fee for chair and propeller is sixty cents an hour, although the chairs may be rented without the guide at a lower rate, in which case a deposit for the safe return of the chair must be left with the man from whose stand it is taken. The chair is returnable to any stand in the grounds, where the deposit is refunded. Many husbands, fathers and lovers avail themselves of the opportunity of pushing a chair in which a frail or loved one is taking a much needed rest. For solid comfort there is nothing to be compared with a great luxurious chair, propelled by a vigorous college youth, who knows not only all the buildings but all the exhibits and is never so happy as when he is dispensing information. Many of the chair guides are college students off for a vacation.

CROWDS AT THE SUNKEN GARDEN.

As a rule the Exposition crowds assemble in the vicinity of some special feature or exhibit. The band stands are sure to be the center of a throng of humanity, for military music appeals to almost every one, whether he be cultivated or not. The Pike and the Plaza of St. Louis are popular because a crowd draws a crowd, and because there is always something going on to attract the nucleus of the crowd. There is one spot in the Exposition that has neither music nor action to recommend it, and yet it is always filled with people. It is the area between the Palaces of Liberal Arts and Mines and Metallurgy, and at the foot of the hill that leads up to the Government Pavilion. This stretch is known as the Sunken Garden, because it is depressed three feet below the level of the surrounding ground. It is framed by sward and broad walks, and from the steps of the Government Pavilion it presents the appearance of a gorgeous piece of tapestry. It is the one bit of gardening that can be taken in as a whole. This is the chief advantage of a sunken garden. The broad walk is lined with benches that are occupied at all hours of the afternoon and evening by World's Fair visitors who are content to spend a little time in the contemplation of pure floral loveliness.

## MISSOURI STATE BUILDING.

The most northern of the group on the Plateau of States, lying directly south of the U. S. Government Building. It is 312 by 160 feet in area, and cost $125,000. To the predominating Roman type of architecture have been added some purely American features. The dome is a perfect hemisphere, gilded and crowned with the magnificent statue of Winged Victory. The central portion of the building is decorated with sculptured groups and single statues of great beauty. A rotunda 76 feet square is the principal interior feature, adjoining an auditorium and reception room seating 1,500 persons. The mantel in this room cost $ 1,000, and in the center of the rotunda is an electric fountain gushing ice water, installed at a cost of S2.000. The building is equipped with a cooling system for use in hot weather. The cost of the sculpture with which the interior and exterior of the building is decorated is over $14,000.

THE ROOSEVELT PRAIRIE CABIN.

The North Dakota exhibit in the Palace of Agriculture consists of two sections, one of which is a conventional booth designed to exploit the resources of the State. The other is unique. It is the cabin, not a reproduction but the cabin itself, in which President Theodore Roosevelt lived from 1883 to 1886 while he was operating a cattle ranch in Northern Dakota. It is an ordinary log cabin of two rooms and is substantially built. The only reminders of the famous man who once occupied it are two pairs of trousers, a hat and a pair of high hunting boots that the ranchman wore almost a score of years before he became President of the United States. On the outer door of the cabin is a silver name plate that was placed there by Miss Alice Roosevelt, eldest daughter of the President, during her visit to the Exposition in the early part of June. On the roof and near the building are some finely mounted specimens of the deer, eagle, owl and fox. On an inner wall is a robe that was tanned, dressed and painted by the Gros Ventre Indians of Fort Berthold reservation. It represents a battle between their chiefs and a band of the Sioux in which the latter were defeated with great slaughter.

## A SNAP-SHOT OF JUDGE PARKER STARTING FOR AN AUTOMOBILE RIDE AT "ROSEMOUNT"

The photograph was taken recently at Rosemont, Judge Parker's home on the Hudson.  It is stated that Judge Parker prefers horseback riding swimming to any other form of exercise.  He also takes an active part in the farm-work on his estate at Esopus.  Up to this time, however, no mention has been made of the addition of automobiling to the daily routine of out-door recreation

### HE RAN AGAINST TEDDY ROOSEVELT

This man had same name but no relation to my grandfather.

# THE EXCITING PIKE

The information about the fair stated that the Pike was one mile long. When the three visitors arrived there, it was teeming with people. Hawkers and barkers were everywhere, trying to lure people into their places of entertainment. Each tried to out-shout the other.

In addition to all the regular activity, there were bands playing, megaphones blasting, and hundreds of voices talking to each other, creating a hum of bee-like noise. A group of dancers from some foreign country were putting on a special show. Everyone was caught up in the excitement.

They walked on down the Pike and the first place that looked interesting was a place called "The Creation". They decided to go in and were put into little boats with other passengers. The boats carried them along and eventually to an area where there was a row of interesting pictures of the creation. Rudy was amazed at the size of the cavern where they were floating. The live ducks in the water made him smile.

After leaving the ride, Rudy looked at Frank with a grin on his face and asked, "Hey, who was that girl you were sitting beside in the boat? You two sure had a long conversation. She's pretty."

Frank fidgeted and cleared his throat. "You forget, my dear brother. Didn't you recognize the beautiful girl who smiled at me when we were on the bridge?"

"Was that the same girl? Geeez! Well, who is she?"

Frank really couldn't wait to tell him. "Get this, Rudy! Mr. McKee, our neighbor is her uncle! Would you call that fate or what? Her name is Grace and she lives on a farm about forty miles from us."

"She appeared to be quite a lady, Frank. Were you properly introduced?" asked Francine.

"No," Frank answered, a little upset. "We were sitting so close and I was only trying to be friendly." Frank was stammering. "Well—I—I just felt I was supposed to know her. Rudy, we've never seen her at Mr. McKee's before because they just moved to that place."

In Francine's social circle, that was never done, but she did not criticize Frank's action. She only commented about how pretty the young lady was.

The three-fairgoers were ready for another ride. They went into a place called "Hereafter". At last, Rudy knew what the people on the ferris wheel were talking about. It was a scary ride, with devils that leaped at you, showing the effects of having to go to Hell and the Lake of Fire. But the last part of a film, about the good people going to Paradise, made the film less frightening.

They saw the animal show, the Fountain of Waters, and ended up going into the building where the babies were in incubators. The name for the little glass houses—incubators—was new to them all. But they thought it was wonderful

People waiting for a parade on the Pike

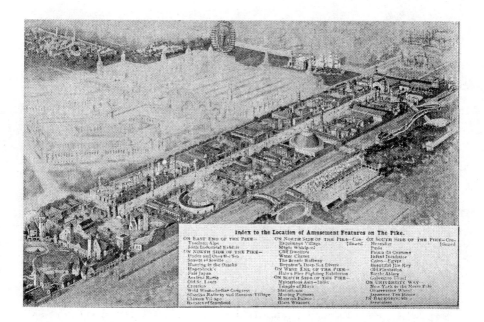

Index to the Location of Amusement Features on The Pike.

## CREATION

The big blue dome marks Creation, one of the elaborate exhibitions on the Pike. The visitor enters a boat that bears him gently away through a labyrinth of underground passages lined with clever scenery. When he disembarks, with a sense of having made a voyage, he finds himself in a roomy cavern where he is diverted by illusions in the form of living heads that seem to have no bodies to support them. He ascends a stairway and comes out upon a revolving platform. Water is before him, in a circular canal. Across the canal are scenes from remote parts of the world. On the water are live ducks and alluring boats. Something or everything is moving -one cannot be certain just what he sees. Down into the cavern the visitor goes again, and up a little stairway he comes, and then he finds himself in one of those very boats—a boat with a cellar stairway. Undoubtedly he is in motion now, but who ever saw a boat with a back staircase? When he has solved the puzzle to his individual satisfaction, he makes his way to the serious part of the exhibition. Seated in a comfortable auditorium, he sees unrolled before his eyes the really glorious pictures of creation as narrated in Genesis.

Grace – the Girl Frank Met.

that someone had invented such a thing. Francine lingered there a long time, and Frank wondered why she and Fred didn't have children.

When they were again outside, Rudy began to scan the area. "That was a wonderful lunch we had earlier, but something I ate made me thirsty."

Frank looked around then pointed toward a man at a refreshment stand. "Look over there. I think I see a man selling drinks."

They wandered toward the man, and to their surprise, he was selling tea. But it was not hot tea—he called it "iced tea". He was from England and when the weather had been so warm, he wasn't able to sell his hot tea. He decided to ice it. Now he was sold out every day, he said. There were also sandwiches there labeled "hot dogs".

"Let's have some iced tea," ventured Francine. "It is always fun to try something new."

The vendor asked did they prefer sugar or lemon? He filled the containers with ice which he chipped from a block of ice with an ice pick, poured in tepid tea, and added the sugar or lemon. None of them had ever heard of such a thing. But they all agreed it was delicious and quite refreshing. Rudy was eyeing the hot dogs.

"It makes one feel cooler," Francine exclaimed. "Now, I can treat my guests to iced tea in warm weather when we entertain. By the way, why don't you two try the hot dogs for lunch tomorrow when you attend the fair?"

Rudy was eager to get to the next ride. "We haven't begun to see all of the Pike. There's an amusement place called the 'Temple of Mirth' that we just can't miss. I heard laughter coming out of there a long way back."

The three entered a doorway to a place filled with happy voices, and they found themselves in a maize of mirrors.

"This is how I will look if I don't watch my eating habits," stated Francine. They giggled and held on to each other and laughed at the distorted reflections of themselves. Francine almost lost her parasol as she was whisked down a circular slide at the end of the attraction. The brothers had gone first, and when they helped her up, hat askew and dress disheveled, she said laughing, "I believe that was one of the best times I've ever had."

The next building housed a reenactment of the Galveston, Texas flood of 1900 in which 6,000 people were drowned. The city had a population of 38,000. They decided it was too depressing and didn't go there.

They went many other places and finally Francine said, "It has been such a wonderful day, but Fred will soon be there for his meal. I prepared some nice cold chicken and potato salad for us tonight. I realize you haven't gotten to your father's exhibit, but since they are doing the judging today, it will be more exciting for you tomorrow."

Rudy's eyes lit up at the sound of food, and he had already learned that if Francine prepared it, it was going to be delicious.

HEREAFTER.

On the south side of the Pike, next to the Paris theater, is the frowning front of "Hereafter," an attraction that is based on Dante's Inferno. The most amusing part of this rather solemn and grewsome spectacle is in the front entrance where the visitor invariably attempts to walk through a mirror, to his own chagrin and the amusement of the other visitors who are waiting for the doors to open. Inside the first theater, the audience is given a bit of spirit materialization that is very cleverly done. Then, following the guide, the audience travels to the outer circle of Hades, crosses the River of Death in Charon's boat and appears before the throne of Minos, one of the three judges of the lower world. From this scene, the guide leads the way to a chamber where the tableau of Faust is shown. Then comes the third circle of Hades in which the wicked are seen frozen yet alive. In the next circle are the wicked who are in the lake of eternal fire, the air around the lake being peopled with demons that leap at the terrified intruders in the realms of the dead. Finally comes the throne room of Satan himself. That is the climax of horrors. From this room the audience passes through the Grove of Daphne to Paradise.

A SCENE FROM "HEREAFTER."

Through rock-ribbed caverns flows the River Styx, while Charon waits to ferry souls across.

BABY INCUBATORS.

One of the most popular concessions on the Pike is that in which the tiny mites of humanity are to be seen. In a handsome building, the back part of which is of fire-proof construction, are fourteen of the finest pattern of infant incubators and a nursery that is all of enamel, nickel and glass. Here the babies from all over the city, that are too trail or too immature at birth to live under natural conditions, are kept in the incubators until they can endure the temperature of the outside air. Then they are transferred to the nursery and are given the most perfect care and are gradually accustomed to the conditions that will surround them in their own homes or the orphan asylums to which they are to be sent. Three physicians, several demonstrators and a corps of trained nurses are always in charge. The demonstrators explain to the visitors just how the incubators are heated and ventilated, and tell a great many interesting and instructive facts about the care of very young children.

In the evening, Frank and Rudy related all that they had seen and done for their brother Fred. They especially enjoyed telling him about Francine's surprise on the slide. He listened intently, happy that the three of them had such a good time together. The food was wonderful; Francine had baked bread the day before, and that with the chicken and potato salad made a very appetizing meal.

Fred was truly interested in what the brothers were doing. "Well, tomorrow is your last day at the fair. What time do you plan to go in the morning, and what will you do?"

"As early as possible," replied Frank. "The judging was today, Francine said. We want to see Pa's exhibit, and there are so many other places we'd like to visit."

That night, it was difficult to close their eyes. "Hey, Frank, are you asleep?"

"No, I was just reflecting on the fine day we've had."

"Of course," answered Rudy, with mirth in his voice, "and you have never once thought of that beauty you were sitting beside in the boat!"

Frank was well aware that he was being teased. "It never entered my mind."

"You know where they say you might go for lying? I'd better take you back to the ride that shows you."

With that, they both laughed and finally drifted off to sleep.

# THE LAST DAY

The morning rose bright and orange-colored. There was a delicious autumn breeze that caused some of the leaves to tremble, then fall. Rudy was awake earlier than anyone, and he rolled over, thinking about their visit with Fred and their days at the fair.

Francine decided to stay home this time, though the brothers implored her to accompany them again. They really enjoyed her company. She declined, saying she wanted to see that they had a nice meal before they left the following day. She also reminded them to try the new sandwich at the fair—the "hot dog".

The grain judging had already taken place, and the sons were eager to get to the Palace of Agriculture to see what had happened.

After arriving at the fairgrounds, Rudy pleaded, "Let's ride one of the Venetian boats to the end of the basin." Frank agreed, and it was a fantastic experience. The gondolier's oaring skills were amazing, and all the while they were on the water, he sang for them. He had a great voice—low and strong and very Italian.

Later, they walked through the model school that had been planned by the government to educate the American Indians. Frank was glad that the country was taking some effort now to care for a culture they had mistreated so badly a hundred years ago and even since.

Rudy was nostalgic. "This is our last day, Frank. I keep looking and looking so I won't forget anything."

As they meandered through the fairgrounds, they chanced upon the balloon rides. Rudy was aghast. "Frank, you don't mean to tell me people go up in those things. Don't they fall?" At that moment, the ropes of a balloon were let loose, and two yelling people sailed into the blue sky.

The attendant of the balloons motioned for the boys to come and take a ride. Frank shook his head, "No siree—that is something I won't do." He thought he had been brave enough when he tackled the ferris wheel. Rudy nodded in complete agreement, and they walked away.

After eating their first delicious "hot dog" at the little stand, Rudy wanted another. But Frank said they were off to the Palace of Agriculture. It was about noon. They entered an immense building of twenty-three acres. It was divided into separate state structures, each displaying all kinds of entries. Besides the grains and crops of every sort, there was art, and handwork, and items too numerous to count. It was very colorful. Some states used different designs—a state flower, or a bird or animal. The walls of a few structures were covered in the grain that was famous in that state. It was all a sight to behold.

It took a lot of walking to find the section for Missouri. As they moved through the crowds, they often stopped to see the offerings of other states. Finally, they saw it—the Missouri display.

The kind of boat Frank and Rudy rode.

GROUP OF AMERICAN INDIANS IN INDIAN CONGRESS.

In the western part of the Exposition grounds, not far from the Philippine Reservation, is the interesting encampment of Indians brought from the various Government reservations. There are about two hundred of these wards of the nation at the Fair. There are twenty-five or more Sioux from the Rosebud Agency, five of whom are shown in the illustration, the men in their war bonnets, and the whole party richly decorated with bead work. In the center stands Tall Crane, and at the left his wife. The Sioux are among the most advanced and interesting of the tribes of American Indians. Originally they occupied the Atlantic coast region, and along the Chesapeake Bay they came into contact with the buffalo and became hunters of the animal, following it toward the West as the herds became lessened. Down the tributaries of the Ohio to the Mississippi the Sioux made their way, the buffalo always their quest and their source of livelihood and wealth. They were the typical Indians of one stage in our country's history, occupying the great plains and opposing the white man's advance. Some of the fiercest battles fought against savages have been those in which the Sioux were engaged, but they were a courageous foe.

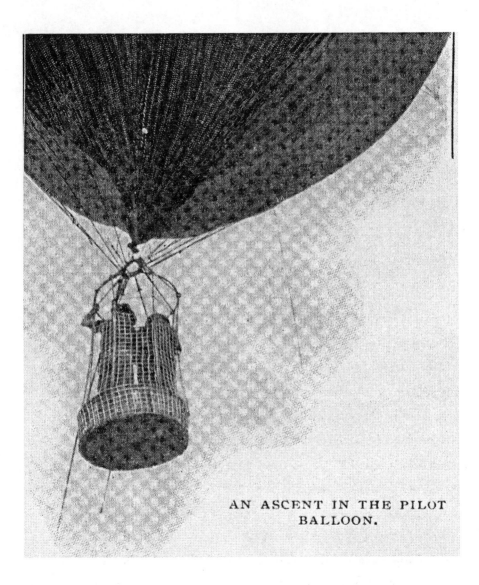

AN ASCENT IN THE PILOT
BALLOON.

TRANSPORTATION AT THE FAIR—AERONAUTICS AT THE FAIR.

A feature of the World's Fair is the great number of balloons and notable experiments with airships. The huge captive balloon is nearly always a conspicuous spot in the sky above the western part of the Exposition, having its station in the Aerial Concourse. On still days the number of passengers going by balloon to a lofty height is as many as the ship can carry, while many go away disappointed in not being able to take the novel ride. The picture on the left shows the basket and a part of the captive balloon. On Liberal Arts day a balloon race for $5,000 was a part of the program. Two balloons entered the race, both of which are seen in the picture on the right. The conditions of the race were that the aeronaut landing nearest the Washington monument in Washington, D. C., should have the prize. It happened that a southeast wind prevailed on the day of the start and the balloons were borne slowly to the northwest, both landing farther from the monument than when starting. For this reason another start was decided upon at a later date and the prize was not awarded.

They both almost ran into the area. Their eyes darted everywhere, seeking the grain competition. At about the same time, they saw the rows of grain entries. Going down the rows, they spied their father's corn. He had named it "Parker's Yellow Dent". And there, in front of the corn, was a silver ribbon. Frank checked again to be sure. Yes, a silver medal had been designated for their father, Henderson Cooper Parker.

The brothers were so excited they could hardly contain themselves. They wanted to leap for happiness. They wanted to shout to the world, "Look here—our Pa did this! Our Pa developed and grew this prize corn!" Instead, they had to be content to stand there and stare at the corn and at the ribbon. Suddenly, something broke loose. They slapped each other's shoulders and laughed and waved their arms wildly. It was almost more than they could believe.

Frank and Rudy realized that Pa didn't get a gold medal, but that was not important. It was such an honor, out of all those entries, to receive a silver one. They had read that the medal itself would be made of heavy polished bronze, about two and a half inches square, and they couldn't wait to take it to him.

They decided to go to the administration office and ask for the award. They took the intramural railway.

"But they haven't been made yet, boys. We're probably not going to be able to mail them all out for a year."

Rudy and Frank hung their heads and their countenances fell. Pa would be so disappointed not to see the medal, even if they told him he'd won it.

The official saw their sad faces. "I'll tell you what. I have some extra medals here that were sent as samples. They are just like the ones that will be made. Suppose I give you one of the silver ones, in its case, and we'll send the certificate with Mr. Parker's name on it when we send the others."

A little shiver went up Frank's spine and he smiled, gratefully. Both brothers shook hands with the kindly man, thanking him again and again. They left the building, medal in hand, knowing it would be a joyous day when they arrived home.

PALACE OF AGRICULTURE.

A single great building covering an area of twenty-three acres is in itself a most interesting object. Such is the Palace of Agriculture, the largest of the Exposition structures. It is in the central western part of the grounds upon a site sixty feet above the main group of buildings, it overlooks, to the northward, the principal group of foreign buildings. On the west side one may see the extensive Philippine Reservation. East are the rose gardens and the southern extension of the Pike. South of it is the Palace of Horticulture. Nearly all the states and nations of the world are here represented. In the central nave are displayed special exhibits of five of the principal products of the soil— corn, cotton, sugar, rice and tobacco. In the southwestern corner is a model dairy in operation. In the center of the building is an extensive refrigerated showcase in which are displayed the dairy products of many states. Here the visitor may see a model creamery in operation using 5000 pounds of milk a day and equipped with all the latest butter and cheese making apparatus. More than two acres are devoted to the food exhibits. In the southeast corner are the agricultural implements and modern farm machinery.

AGRICULTURAL EXHIBIT OF THE STATE OF MISSOURI.

This is where Cooper's corn was exhibited.

354. California's Exhibit of Fruit.

No. 12 "Lone Star" of Texas, Made of Grain

No. 21. Louisiana's State Exhibit.

To show the size of the Palace of Agriculture

# HOME WITH PA

The brothers were on the train, traveling back to Kidder, Missouri. They were both quiet, each reveling in his own thoughts about their ethereal time in St. Louis. Every so often, Frank touched his upper pocket to be sure Pa's medal was still there. Rudy checked for his violin.

Fred and Francine had been very excited that Fred's father won the medal. They were going to put a notice in the paper, but the Fair would probably do that anyway. It gave Fred new insight into his father's life, and he understood more now about his family. Francine had stated again that she hoped they could visit the Parker family in the spring. Fred agreed that it had been too long since he had seen his Pa.

The train finally chugged into the station where Pa was awaiting his sons with the horse and buggy. White steam spewed forth as the engine slowed to a stop, which frightened Mabel a little. Again Frank touched the medal in his pocket. They were certain Pa hadn't heard a thing.

Pa greeted them with a big smile. He was anxious to hear all the news. It was very difficult to keep from just rushing up and telling Pa about the medal. But the sons had already decided to wait until they arrived home. They kept him from asking questions by talking of Fred and Francine, about how much they liked Fred's wife, and that the two of them were going to visit in the spring. They told him every detail of their fabulous home-cooked meals and also about Fred's gift of the violin to Rudy.

When it looked like Pa was going to again ask a question, they quickly continued with information on the trolley they rode, the cars they saw—including Fred's new one--, about the goods in the store windows, and they told Pa that they had ridden on streets covered with tar.

They could stall a long time with all of the information on the fair. Pa heard about the blue waterways and the boats; he marveled at the story of the balloon rides and the rides on the Pike. They continued on talking of the statues, the white buildings, the electric lights. Frank even disclosed his feelings about the beautiful ladies he'd seen—just to keep Pa busy. Then he told him that Mr. McKee's niece was going to visit her uncle at Thanksgiving time.

At last, the buggy pulled into the farmyard. Home looked so good to Rudy. He couldn't wait to sleep in his own bed again. He had been extremely comfortable at Fred's, but this was home.

Pa had fixed a small supper for them, and it tasted good. They were both quite hungry after their long journey on the train.

"All right", began Pa, "I been waitin' long enough. My patience is wearing thin. I've been listin' to all the excitin' chatter about Fred and Francine and the fair. I feel I have almost riddin' the trolley, the ferris wheel, and most of the boats. Will you please tell me about the judgin'?"

Train like this homeward

PALACE OF ELECTRICITY.

A very large building is devoted to the exhibits of the Department of Electricity. Including the court, the building covers eight acres and the cost was $400,000. The groups of lofty columns about the entrances and their classic details give the building a dignity worthy of its central position in the "main picture" of the Exposition. The exhibits in the Palace of Electricity will make it a center of attraction for all who are concerned in electrical progress. The remarkable advance in electrical engineering and the new discoveries of the science during the last ten years made possible the most comprehensive exhibit ever assembled. Dynamos and motors of many kinds and new electrical machinery for a multitude of uses may be seen in operation. Definite progress has been made during recent years in the use of electricity in the treatment of diseases. How it is thus used is illustrated with X-ray apparatus and the famous Finsen light. The progress in electric lighting and the use of electric power is shown. Small but powerful electric locomotives for mining purposes make an interesting exhibit. The wonders of electro-chemistry are illustrated.

## FESTIVAL HALL AND GRAND BASIN.

The view shown is one of the majestic sweeps of the Cascade Gardens and their settings. At the left rises the dome of Festival Hall, 200 feet above the crown of the hill on which it stands. Rich carpets of sward slope gracefully down toward the waters of the Grand Basin, and the wonderful rainbow gardening makes a picture not to be excelled elsewhere. The observer contemplating this scene faces nearly west. The western arm of the Colonnade of States connects Festival Hall with the restaurant pavilion near the center of the picture. The ever-charming cascade at the west shows clearly, though the great central cascade can be better seen from the Grand Basin. Toward the right, the 250-foot circle of the Observation Wheel is sharply defined against the sky, and at the extreme right a portion of the Palace of Machinery may be seen. A part of the white walls of Jerusalem peers over the hill. The scene is one of majesty, of vastness, of many objects combined into a satisfying and harmonious whole. It fills the eye, and delights with a wealth of color and grace of line, and charms with the swirl and play of water. The surface of the basin ripples and dapples under the wind and the sun, and to complete the satisfaction of the beholder the sounds of music and of voices add the human note.

Fountain in the Grand Basin

## PALACE OF ELECTRICITY.

A very large building is devoted to the exhibits of the Department of Electricity. Including the court, the building covers eight acres and the cost was $400,000. The groups of lofty columns about the entrances and their classic details give the building a dignity worthy of its central position in the "main picture" of the Exposition. The exhibits in the Palace of Electricity will make it a center of attraction for all who are concerned in electrical progress. The remarkable advance in electrical engineering and the new discoveries of the science during the last ten years made possible the most comprehensive exhibit ever assembled. Dynamos and motors of many kinds and new electrical machinery for a multitude of uses may be seen in operation. Definite progress has been made during recent years in the use of electricity in the treatment of diseases. How it is thus used is illustrated with X-ray apparatus and the famous Finsen light. The progress in electric lighting and the use of electric power is shown. Small but powerful electric locomotives for mining purposes make an interesting exhibit. The wonders of electro-chemistry are illustrated.

Pa's Silver Medal made of bronze

This is a second-place medal.

Frank reached in his pocket and pulled out the case that housed the medal. He handed it to his father. Pa just held it and looked at Frank, puzzled. Then he lifted the lid. His eyes widened and all he could say softly was "Oh My!—Oh! My!"

When Pa finally caught his breath, he stammered, "But—but—Frank, there were so gosh many entries. Are you certain this was awarded to the Yellow Dent Corn?"

Frank smiled and reassured him. "The fair administrator gave it to us himself, Pa. He said he will send your certificate later." Frank and Rudy stood beside their father, feeling great happiness. They could only guess what their father was experiencing.

Pa took the medal out of its case. He turned it over and over. He read the inscriptions, then he read them again. All the while, the tears were trickling down his weathered cheeks. His many efforts and years of work had meant something at last. He had been awarded a second highest for his hybrid corn. How proud he was that he could now make two grains of corn grow on an ear, where one grew before. He had almost doubled the yield.

Frank patted his father's shoulder and said, "We're awful proud of you, Pa." Rudy echoed Frank's words.

They motioned to each other to go upstairs to bed—to leave Pa to enjoy his time of triumph.

---

"Hey, Frank, are you still awake?"

"There's no way, Rudy, I could be asleep yet."

"Ma must be awful proud of Pa tonight," Rudy continued.

Frank lay comfortably in his favorite oak bed—thinking of many things, including Grace's visit in the fall. "I'm sure she is proud of him, Rudy. She is aware of the work that went into this task. It's part her medal too."

"Didn't we have a wonderful time, Frank?"

"The best, Rudy. I can't think of anyone I'd rather go to a fair with than you—except maybe one of those pretty ladies."

Rudy smiled. "The way I see it, Frank, you might have a pretty lady to go with yourself next time. I suppose then you will leave me at home."

"No, you can go along too. We'll just meet you later at the ferris wheel." Frank stifled a laugh.

"You mean—you'll want to be alone. Okay, Frank, I can take a hint."

Rudy grinned and rolled over in his bed. Something in his chest felt like it was going to burst. He guessed it was pride. He was proud of his family, proud of Frank for his care, proud of Pa for his hard work. And he was glad his family would be extended now with a visit from Fred and Francine.

"As the ferris wheel turns--," he thought sleepily. "As the ferris wheel rolls on—just like life does—we'll see more good times together." His eyes closed, and he found himself dreaming of his ride on the big wheel. He sighed and smiled in his sleep.

# SUGGESTED TOPICS FOR RELATED STUDY

Book:  MEET ME AT THE FERRIS WHEEL
(For further research and advanced work)
by: Joy Dawson

1. Planning for the St. Louis World's Fair of 1904, celebrating the Louisana Purchase Centennial

   a. Procuring the land and making plans

   b. Constructing the buildings

   c. Planning for millions of visitors

   d. Contacting foreign countries

   e. Dediction of the Fair at the Liberal Arts Building

   f. Setting up exhibits and awards

   g. The Pike and its amusements

   h. The large pipe organ in Festival Hall on the fairgrounds

   i. Transportation on the fairgrounds

   j. Foods of today—made popular and sold at the Fair

2. Farm life in the early 1900's

   a. Food cultivation and preservation

   b  Keeping warm in winter

   c. Water sources for farm life

   d. Plumbing and sanitation methods

   e. Lighting in the home in the 1900's

   f. Transportation in a rural area

   g. Homesteading land--how it was done

3. Thomas Edison, inventor of the electric light—his role in the 1904 Fair

4. The "Liberty Bell" at the Fair and its history

5. President Theodore Roosevelt and his involvement at the Fair

6.  The Lewis and Clark Expedition

7.  The Louisana Purchase

8.  The life of Louis Joliet or Hernando de Soto

9.  General Ulysses S. Grant, his life and his log cabin at the Fair

10. Abraham Lincoln's railroad car at the Fair and trains of 1900's

11. Cars at the time of the "Parade of Automobiles" at the Fair

12. "Hot-Air Ballooning" at the time of the Fair

13. Mr. Ferris and his invention of the ferris wheel

14. 1904 World's Fair Olympics

15. Japanese bonsai trees at the Fair and how they are grown and pruned

16. Patagonia Indians, location, origin and culture

# About the Author

Joy Dawson lived for two short periods of time in the very house her grandfather built (see picture inside). The story comes from accounts given her by her father, Rudy and Frank, her uncle. She has embellished the events when there was no information to be had, even using some of her own experiences while living in the old farmhouse, but much of the story is true. The facts about the fair come from relatives and from personal research.

Joy has had a long teaching career in English, drama and reading; reared four sons; has eight grandchildren and four great-grandchildren. Her interest in the 1904 World's Fair stems from her grandfather's corn entry for the state of Missouri and from the great developments of that period of history

Printed in the United States
47492LVS00005B/253-402